A Road to
NOWHERE

NAEYLA EL-HAJJ

To order additional copies of this book, contact:
Bookwhip
1-855-339-3589
https://www.bookwhip.com

CHAPTER 1

"**H**urry up man we're gonna be late," Sean grumbled to his best friend.

"Since when are you worried about the time?" His friend asked him as he slowly admired his looks in the mirror.

"I'm not worried about the time. I just want you to hurry up," Sean heaved.

There was a new movie out that week and they wanted to get the best seats. They thought that the best seats were in the front, even though it was a big screen. Sean stood there for at least five minutes waiting for his friend to hurry up.

"Are we gonna stand here all night with you staring at me like that? Come on lets go," his friend replied. Sean was about to reply but caught himself and didn't want to say anything.

"You're weird you know that?"

"You're the one that was standing in the middle of the mirror. I wasn't."

They both laughed as they walked downstairs. They were silent as they walked passed the kitchen with Sean's mom in there. They didn't say a word until they left the house.

The breeze was slow and calm and drifted in and out. There was something about the stillness that seemed to have drifted out that evening. The sky switched from a sky blue to an evening pink. Quickly as it came, the colour faded only into a dark colour that everyone always ignored.

As soon as they got to the theater they quickly got there stuff and went to the room where the movie was playing. Someone quickly passed by coming from the wrong direction and almost bumped into them.

"Sorry." They quickly ran to the other direction.

Finally they got into their seats and soon as they sat, they waited for the movie to end. They went and watched another movie and left after it finished. There was small talk between them.

"How did you like the movie?" his friend replied.

"It wasn't too bad. Did you like it?"

"Sort of. It got boring in the end."

"Yeah. It sort of just dragged on," Sean agreed with him.

"The other movie that we just watched was better."

"Yeah. Probably because it was scarier." They laughed at the small joke. Their talk turned to a small hum that sounded like two mosquitoes that were waiting for the right time to sting. It lingered in the air for a while and drifted off.

As they drove off, Sean thought that they were being followed as he saw a car drive behind them. He quickly faked a turn only to find that the car wasn't following them.

"What did you do that for?" his friend answered looking behind them only to find no one there.

"Someone was following us," he stared through the rearview mirror once more and saw that no one was following them. There was a moment of silence between them.

"Some night huh?" His friend thought aloud. Sean quickly agreed with him. The car that was behind them, sped into the night. Without a trace of heat trailing behind and without a car in front or behind him, the car made its way through.

He grabbed a tight hold on to the steering wheel as his hands were losing grip. He was glad that he lost the wailing noise of the siren as the police were after him. He remembered taking his ex- girlfriend's car after she dumped him. Now she was after him again only to get her car back. He knew that she was never going to get it.

There wasn't a chance she was ever going to get it back, not in a million years. He followed a car in front of him keeping a good distance away from the car. The car finally slowed down a bit, turned a corner, and stopped in front of the first house.

After the car had left, he turned the corner to watch one of his other ex-girlfriends who stopped in the driveway and started crying. He didn't like seeing her like that. He got out of his car and walked up to her. He smiled warmly at her. She looked up at him, recognized his face, and backed away from him. She looked around her to see if anyone was watching. She ran towards her house trying to unlock the door.

Seeing her run, he knew that she made a mistake. He made a change of plans as he went after her, trying to get a hold of her. She tried struggling in his grasp. Each time she did, his grip tightened around her. She tried screaming only she couldn't because he had one hand on her mouth.

She moved under his grasp trying to kick him where it hurts. But he knew what she was up to and his reflexes were fast enough to catch her body movements. He dragged her away from the door as the lights inside were put on and led them the way to his car. She could do nothing but wait until the cops and her parents find her. She was desperate and in need to scream only she couldn't because he wouldn't let her.

The next morning, Sean was too tired to get out of bed. His alarm rang in the morning to wake him up. Instead, he hit the snooze button hard and dragged himself deeper into the bed. It was the only day he had off of work and he just wanted to sleep in. He was in a heavy sleep that he didn't feel the covers slip off him. He tried grabbing the covers, but he only grabbed thin air. He dropped his arm and forgot about the covers.

With one arm dangling on one side of the bed and his other arm on his chest he snored away forgetting about everything that happened in the last couple of days. He felt his cat moving beside him and snuggled beside his head. At the same moment, he felt ice cold water splash him in the face. He tried waking up to see what was going on. When he opened his eyes, more water was splashed him again.

"Hey come back here," Sean cried.

He tried untangling himself as he got up. He got tired just doing that. When he was finally out of the mess, he ran after his cousin. He stumbled after him and tripped as he stepped out of the doorway. His cousin just stood there laughing at him holding the cat. It squirmed in his arms and meowed loud. Finally, he let the cat go and it ran back into Sean's room. Just as Sean was about to get up, his cousin pushed him from behind and he fell down.

"I'm going to get you one day. So you better watch your back," Sean cried.

"Ooh I'm so scared," his cousin made a face at him.

Sean just made a face back at him. Just then his mom came walking in the hallway to see what the commotion was all about. Sean looked up to see his mom was all dolled up for something or someone.

"What are you doing there sitting on the floor? Get up and get dressed," his mom was shocked.

"For what, your wedding?" Sean replied looking at his mom.

"What are doing dressed up like that? I hope you're not planning on going anywhere with someone. Are you?" Sean contradicted his mom. He got up and faced her.

"I don't have time for this Sean. And yes I am going somewhere and that's none of your business."

"Why not? It is actually my business and I tend to know where you are going," Sean was almost shouting. He was definitely awake. He stood up and glared his mom down.

"You are not the man of this house you know that." She stared downstairs.

"Oh and exactly who is? Tell me mom 'cause I can just go around every neighborhood and ask the dozens of men if they are the man of this house. So I want to know exactly where you are going." Sean's cousin stood in the hallway listening to their conversation.

"I don't have time for this please move. I have a meeting that I have to go to and I'm going to be late." She stared continuously at the floor. She didn't want to look him in the face when he got angry it just made her sad. He didn't move out of her way. He stood there for less than a minute not even thinking.

"Really. You have a meeting huh?" Sean stormed into his room, quickly put his clothes on that he wore the day before, not caring. He stared at his mom for a moment and stormed out slamming the front door behind him. His mom stood there shaking in her high heels.

She went back to her room and stared at herself in the mirror. Her eyes were streaked with mascara and eye shadow, her face was plump with blush. She didn't like seeing Sean depressed this way, she didn't even like looking at the sight of him when he got angry. She hoped that he wasn't going to do anything stupid. She cried deep inside and the pain was hurting where it always hurts. She looked back in the mirror to see that her eyes were bloodshot.

"Aunt Rose are you okay?" She turned towards the door and smiled at him.

"I'm fine. Why don't you go to the neighbour's house and play there for a while?" He didn't object so he left with a still smile.

She watched him leave with a small frown on his face. She sat there in front of her mirror deciding whether or not if she should leave. She knew that Sean always got back into his regular mood. She took on that dreary look once again before she went to the bathroom to fix her makeup and quickly left without leaving a note to Sean.

Inside, the lights were packed bright. Footsteps pounded on the stairs, the shouts and laughter bounced off the walls.

"Bye mom," Heather shouted.

"Bye sweetie. Be careful. When I go upstairs I expect to see the lights turned off in your rooms," her mom shouted. Their laughter rang again. Heather walked quickly towards the car and jumped in.

"About time man. Geeze, I thought you were never gonna come," Josh replied.

"Why wouldn't I come? I would never miss this concert for anything," Heather laughed.

"Yeah right." Sean, who was always in his upbeat mood, had a weary look on his face.

"What's up with you man?" Josh asked him. Sean just ignored him and tried to ignore everything. He reached up in the front and blared the car with music to drown out his mothers' voice in his head. David stared at him through the rearview mirror with a look that knew what was going on.

When they reached the stadium, they can see from the parking lot that it was already packed. They quickly jogged their way up to try to get to their seats.

"Who is the best band in the world?" Josh cried.

"WESTLIFE," Sean, David, and Billy shouted. They all laughed happily. Other's turned to see what the commotion was. David and Tracy walked behind their friends. David held on to Tracy's hand and smiled at her. When they reached the stadium, it was already packed. Some of the stayed behind with a good view, the others, made their way to the front. David stayed silent for a while and held on to Tracy's hand as he led them to their spots right in the front by the stage.

"Did anybody see David and Tracy?" Billy shouted over the noise.

"Who cares about them anyways," Sarah screamed. They all looked at each other and shook their heads. They looked around to see if they were anywhere. They didn't bother looking for them, so they forgot about them and enjoyed the concert.

They were all into the concert, that they forgot about the time and didn't know exactly what time the it ended. They only wished that the concert went all night. Once they left, they were still psyched about it. Sean and Josh still wondered where David and Tracy were.

"Who cares? At least we get to drive all night without Tracy whining about going home early for no reason," Sarah said bitterly.

They all stared at her, Heather silently agreed with her. Even though Heather liked Tracy, she didn't want Sarah to know because she didn't want to choose over whom she liked the best. Heather put a small smile on her face when she saw Tracy and David walking far behind them. Their conversation was erupted with laughter. They turned to see them trailing behind.

"Did you see the look on his face when I asked him that?" David laughed.

"Yeah. He looked like he wanted to punch you. You should have told Marc about Sean. I think that they would make a great couple." Tracy laughed hard.

"I agree. Let me see the picture." Tracy couldn't stop laughing.

"What were you trying to do?"

"I don't know it got messed up. I took another picture it turned better see," he switched to the next picture.

"That's better I like that one better." They slowed their pace and stared at the pictures.

"Wait go back."

"What?"

"I love this picture. You know why because I took it." She waved her hands on the front of the camera and gently touched the screen. There was a long moment of silence. David stared at Tracy with a soft smile on his face while she looked through the other pictures. He wrapped his arms around her.

"I love you, you know that?"

"Yes I do." Tracy replied. He brought his lips to hers and kissed her softly. Tracy went back to the first picture and laughed.

"You're so weird you know that."

"I know. It's the best compliment that I got so far."

"It wasn't meant to be." They turned to see David and Tracy walking up to them.

"Where were you guys?" Billy wondered.

"We were in the front. To bad you guys weren't there with us," David shouted and smiled at them. Sean who was quiet the whole time, smiled at them and their enthusiasm. Sean knew exactly where they were. He got them their tickets and their seats were in the front. He also got them backstage passes. No one knew but him and Heather. They both ran towards the car and laughed at each other. As they got in, they waited for their friends who were walking as slow as ever.

"You guys are so slow," David cried when they reached the car. When they all got in, they screamed their loudest until heads were turned from directions and Billy plugged his ears.

"Geeze, man. What's wrong with you guys?" Josh, who was sitting beside Sarah, screamed the loudest out of all of them. She had to plug her ears.

"What's wrong with you? Can't have a little fun?" Josh taunted him. Sarah and Heather looked at each other and just shook their heads.

"Now that was a concert. Don't you think?" Josh replied in the back.

"Hell ya man," David watched him in the rearview mirror. The stereo was tuned up and blared all night as they drove around until they got tired. Tracy began to grow tired afterwards, and the rest of them all grew tired. Sarah rolled her eyes at them as their eyes began to droop.

"Do you wanna go somewhere after this?" Sarah leaned in toward Heather who covered a yawn with the back of her hand.

"It's really late and I promised my mom I'd be home as soon as the concert finished." Heather looked at her. She wasn't trying to be mean, she was telling the truth. She watched Sarah roll her eyes at her and drew away from her. When David stopped by her house to drop her off, she jumped out before he could even stop. When she was out of earshot they all blew in a sigh of relief.

"What's wrong with her?" Josh asked. Billy looked like he was about to cry.

"I don't know. I don't know." That was all he said and everything grew calm for them. They were happy and upbeat and relieved that they went to the concert. It was a lot better for Heather and Tracy now that Sarah was gone. They were just glad that they were having the best time of their life. Until then, the music and their laughter was the only thing that brightened up the darkness.

CHAPTER 2

The next morning, seemed brighter than the day before. The morning dragged by quickly eager to get things done. Tracy was surprised to see her parents in the afternoon. They were barely inside as she raced to hug them.

"Happy birthday Tracy," her mom replied as they were completely inside the house.

"Thanks mom." Her mom stared at the house with a look that said she was happy that she didn't have to clean the house all the time.

"Wow it's pretty clean," her mom inspected half the house. She walked into the kitchen to find nothing on the countertops. She put some stuff down on the shelves and raised some questions toward Tracy.

"What have you been doing to keep yourself company?"

"Nothing," Tracy added with a smile.

"Are you sure?" Her mom winked at her.

"Yes."

"Why don't we go out and find a place to eat?" her dad suggested.

"I think that would be a good idea. It will all do us some good." As Tracy and her mom went upstairs she asked her mom if it was because it was her birthday.

"Don't be silly. We just never get to spend enough time with you," her mom hugged her once again. Tracy missed her mom's arms around her. She held onto her for a while.

"We better hurry up before your dad has a fit and sees us still standing here," her mom responded and they both laughed before they went upstairs to change. They were all out of their morning clothes and dressed in their afternoon clothes before they left. Her dad never had the time to take them out anywhere for dinner. The last time she remembered her dad taking them out, was when she was about five years old.

It still felt a bit odd, as they had just came down for her birthday. They rarely ever came to town. If they did, it was either for a few short hours, or for the night and left in the morning. It was still a surprise to Tracy that he was willing to do something like that.

As they arrived at the restaurant, Tracy was stunned to see how expensive everything was. She beamed happily at her mom and her mom smiled back. As they got their seat and ordered for their food, her dad decided to give her the present.

"What is it?" Tracy just stared at the tiny box.

"Open it and see," her dad smiled and turned his gaze on his wife. They both leaned back and watched Tracy open it. She lifted the lid carefully. When she opened it, she was shocked to see what it was. She traced her fingers on the diamonds of the necklace. Also, she found a tiny imprint in the box and on the back of the necklace. She just sat there stunned and happy not knowing what to say. Both her parents laughed when she couldn't even take the words out of her mouth.

"Are you serious?" She finally replied in a small blow of breath.

"Do you like it?" Her dad sat back and waited for her next reaction.

"Are you kidding? I love it. Thanks mom thanks dad you're the best." She hugged them both.

"I saw it in the window and it was the same one you wanted a while ago."

"The one that you wouldn't let me get. Remember that?"

"Yes I do. And I knew that you wanted it so bad. So I got it for you for a better price than it was before." He watched her putting it on, and fingered it as it fell perfectly into place around her neck.

"How much was it?"

"Just as long as you love it, you do not need to ask me that question." They all laughed.

"I really love it. It's the best."

"We're glad that you like it," her mom smiled. Just as their food came her dad sighed.

"Finally. I was beginning to wonder if we were the only ones that aren't starving."

They stared at some people who were still waiting for their food and Tracy laughed. Just before they ate, her dad made a toast.

"To the wonders of all the things that can happen and to Tracy," their glasses clicked and their laughter rang out far more than it ever has. It took them almost an hour to leave and drive back home.

They walked inside with laughter and smiles on their faces. Just then, her dad explained to her that they both had to make leave for work that night.

"Will you be okay home alone," her mom gave an expression of worry.

"Yeah. I'll be fine don't worry about it. I've been home alone before it's no big deal," Tracy grinned.

Her mom smiled back at her. They hugged once again and said happy birthday once again before they left. Tracy stood in front of the doorway with a smile where they stood for less than five minutes and made it all last as a memory that she wanted to keep forever in her heart. She closed her eyes and smiled at the thoughts that were running through her mind.

She made her way into the kitchen, happy to find an excuse not to worry about anything at all. When she reached the landing at the bottom of the stairs, the doorbell rang. She walked slowly towards it and opened it. She breathed in a silence of relief when it was only David.

"What's wrong," he gave in to that frown that she had but it quickly faded into a smile.

"Nothing. I just thought you were someone else. That's all," she replied when he gave a worried look.

"Are you sure?" he played with her thoughts.

"Yes I'm sure."

"Come on I want to show you something." She closed the door, took his hand in hers, and went up to her room. When they were in her room, he closed the door.

"I want to give you something," he replied.

"Can't it wait? I'm sure we can wait for the rest of them to come." Tracy smiled.

"Well this is something special that can't wait," David replied taking out a small tiny box out of his pocket.

"Open it." He watched her take it in her hands and admired it for a while. When she opened it, her face took on a surprising look before she turned her gaze back to David.

"You like it? I got it especially for you. Look here, there's an engravement behind it. See." He held it in front of her with his hands shaking a bit. But he hid it not wanting her to see that. He waited for a while to know what she was thinking.

"You don't like it?" his smile turned into a frown. She looked back up at him as if he had said the stupidest thing.

"No of course not I love it. It's the best thing I've gotten so far. Including this necklace actually," she fingered the necklace in front of him.

"It's beautiful. But not as beautiful as you." David looked at the diamonds that shone in the light and looked up at her.

"My parents got it for me."

"Yeah I can tell." He looked deep in her eyes and at that moment, they were able to hear each other's thoughts and what they felt inside. His gaze turned softer and brought his lips to hers. His lips grazed softly against hers.

Letting him take control, she found herself against the wall as he ground his hips gently into hers. David's lips moved to her jawline then her neck, eliciting a moan from his kisses. Tracy moved her fingers to undo one button at a time to touch his skin. David moved his lips back to hers and kissed her with deep passion and lust. With a final kiss, he let go and their foreheads touched, their breathing ragged.

"I have one more thing for you."

"Really?"

"Really. But it can wait until everybody leaves." David chuckled.

"I can't wait." She whispered.

"I love you."

"I love you too." He kissed her one last time, before they went downstairs. They walked into the den and heard heavy footsteps stumbling in.

"Hey, Tracy. Am I the first one?" Josh cried out stumbling in drunk. He walked around for a while before he was able to know where he was going. He walked into the den to find Tracy and David sitting there watching television.

"What's the matter with you?" David stared at Josh with a stunned look on his face.

"I…I…I was running like…like craz…crazy from my house. I…I don't kno…know what got over me," Josh threw himself on to the couch gasping for breath. He wheezed like a baby. Tracy ran upstairs to get him some water. She sat beside him and put her arms around him.

"Are you okay?" she just stared at him. He gasped for breath before he was able to talk.

"I'll be …ine." He wheezed and tumbled on his words. Their gazes turned toward the television.

"That wasn't funny you know," Josh finally said without difficulty after ten minutes of silence. To ease in some better conversation rather than lingering on one thing, Josh changed the subject.

"What wasn't funny?" David smiled at Tracy.

"The way you were here before me."

"It wasn't meant to be."

"Whatever man," Josh ignored him and turned to Tracy.

"What do you think David got you?" He winked.

"Yeah I don't think you need me anymore," Tracy went and sat beside David. She just shook her head and ignored him. They both stared at Josh as his smile widened at the both of them. Tracy gave a heavy sigh and left.

"Would you get me some more water? Thanks you're a doll," Josh replied reaching his arm out with the cup in his hand without giving her time to think.

"I'm sure you could get it yourself now that you're feeling better."

"Aww. That's no way to talk to me," he got up and walked towards her, she dodged away from him and left.

"Did you see what she just did to me? She ran away from me." David laughed at him.

"It's not funny you know. She won't even let me hug her and it's her birthday."

"It's probably because you're disgusting." David chuckled. Tracy snuck a peak at them. Josh saw her and ran after her. They both stopped at the front of the door struggling with each other and saw Billy and Sean coming in.

"What the hell are you doing?"

"I'm trying to hug her but she won't let me."

"It's probably because you're disgusting," Sean repeated and he and Billy both laughed.

"Now where were we?" Josh turned around to find Tracy gone. He walked into the den and saw them all sitting there.

"What's with you?" Sean asked him.

"He's high on drugs. I see him take them every night," Billy laughed. Josh mocked him. "You know nothing of me," Josh threw himself on an empty couch.

"Yeah right your blood is in mine as is mine is in yours which makes me your brother. So technically I know you. Your room is across from mine." They all stared at Josh who looked confused.

"Whatever man." He turned away from them and tried to do something productive. That evening passed by quickly with the five of them doing something and waited for Sarah and Heather to come. They finally came when it was past the time Tracy wanted them to come at.

"What took you so long?" David asked. Sarah didn't answer him; she just reached over for a chip from the bowl on the table.

"Car was running low?" Heather shrugged looking at Sarah. He nodded his head not sure if he was to believe them or not.

"Are we going to get this party started or what?" was all Billy had to say to get the music and the party started. Heather and Sarah found other ways to amuse themselves. They stared at Tracy who was having fun. After ten minutes, Sarah and Heather left. As Billy went to call them he found them leaving.

"Why are you leaving?"

"This place is junk we're gonna go somewhere else." Billy stared at Sarah with a disgusting look on his face. He stared at Heather who was on the verge of tears. He didn't know what to do. Billy just went back to the living room.

"So where are they?" David asked.

"They left," he just shrugged. Tracy hid the tears and the anger inside and kept a smile on her face.

"Why did we have to leave?" They sat in the car watching the light inside grow brighter.

"I can't stand her. I don't know why I even came." Heather didn't want to say anything that would get Sarah mad. They heard their laughter and their screams. Sarah couldn't stand their laughter. They left as soon as they could.

He tried to picture himself walking in on them and killing them all. He pictured their bodies on top of each other as he ripped their garments off and their guts were piled up beside each other. He could even picture blood dripping wet from the ceiling as confetti, and their lungs hanging and blown up in balloons. He got the shivers just thinking of that. Oh how much he wanted to do it. If only he had the chance to do it, he would. He could picture them once again. If only he could, if only he could.

CHAPTER 3

"**O**kay, this is what happened," Billy replied during dinner.

"I thought the party was over because everyone was leaving, but they didn't pack up or call their brothers and sisters. So I thought they forgot something. Turned out, that they left for another party and it got worse at that point," Billy finished off.

"What happened after that, you call for help?" Dylan said laughing. Billy kicked him in the leg.

"Ow," he cried.

"I've got better news. My boss gave me a ten dollar raise," Josh said casually covering Billy's news. His parents congratulated him. Billy stared at him through his glasses with a stern look on his face until dinner ended. Billy and Josh took over the kitchen as dinner ended.

"Ow. What was that for man?" Billy jumped. Josh just laughed at him. Billy punched him back.

"Ow. Fuck man that hurt," Josh cried.

"There. At least we're even," Billy exclaimed laughing.

"Ha ha, you're funny," Josh took a quick hold of him.

"Are you guys done yet?" Dylan asked coming into the kitchen.

"No. We just started," Josh announced.

"Well hurry up then." He stomped out of the kitchen. When he was quickly out of earshot, they both wrestled with each other.

After waiting an hour, Dylan got impatient. He walked into the kitchen to find his brothers leaving.

"Tell mom and dad we left," Josh replied taking a piece of cake from Dylan. He cried out in alarm.

"What if I don't?"

"Well then I guess we're just bigger men than you are." They both left before he could reply. Dylan just shrugged and went to go get another piece of cake and went to go watch television.

There was a long moment of silence between Sean and his mother. They were both sitting in the living room with the television on. Not a word was spoken. Sean left the room and went to his bedroom. He didn't know what to do. He loved his mom yet at the same time he didn't. It didn't make sense to him that way, it was confusing.

He shrugged off the feeling inside of him. He was about to leave when he saw his mom leave with somebody. He was on the verge of throwing something against the wall. He hated the things that he saw and he hated the things that he heard. He hated what his mother told most people about him. He went back to his room looking at pictures and thinking over things that have gone wrong in his life.

"When are you going to ever learn? It's only just a joke," his mom told him once. But it wasn't a joke to him. He wanted to do something that would make him regret it for doing it. He wanted his mom to regret the day that he was born and the mistakes that she made and the things that she said and did to him.

"Don't do this right now. I have to go to work," his mom replied one day when he was little.

"It's not fair mommy. I want to know." He kept asking her questions. She knew he wasn't going to give up he wanted to know everything. When she knew that he wasn't going to stop she slapped him across the face, which made her cry for a week and she never came out of her room.

Almost everyday his mom never came home. He would have to make dinner for himself. Most of the time she was sitting in her room with a gloomy face staring at nothing that never seemed right to her at all. He caught her once in his room staring at the pictures when they used to be together and when he used to have the smile on his face that she loved.

He gasped with tears streaming down his face and his mom gazed up and saw him standing there in the doorway. Her face streaked with tears and her eyes bloodshot red without any makeup. He noticed tears streaming down her face. That was the first time she ever smiled at him.

"I have to tell you something," she had told him a couple of years ago. There was one thing that his mom never told him and she had to tell him because he was going to have to find out eventually.

"What is it mom? Is it one of those guys? 'Cause I swear I'm gonna rip their heads off."

"No. Just listen to me. I haven't told you this. And I know that I should've told you a long time ago when this happened."

"What? Tell me." She took a deep breath.

"You have a brother." It was all she said to make him scream. When his mom left later that evening to go to work (which he knew she obviously went somewhere else), he found papers strewn on the table that gave him every information about his brother. He couldn't believe that he had a brother. Of all those years, she didn't even bother to tell him anything about it at all. It has been four years since that time. He wasn't going to forget the things that his mom told him.

In the midst of his thoughts he heard the phone ring. He ignored the phone. It kept on ringing until he finally answered.

"Hello?"

"I hope you're having fun right now Sean. Please tell me you are 'cause I'm watching you. I know who you are and I want you to show me your face. Why don't you come outside and I can show you who I am." The voice barely came out. It was a low whisper that didn't sound like a voice at all.

"Who is this? David is that you?"

"David? My name is not David. My name is........" There was a noise in the background and he couldn't make it out.

"I'm coming for you Sean so you better watch your back." In an instant the line became dead and there was no one on the other line.

"Hello. Hello?" There was no answer. The only thing that he could hear was the dial tone. He hung up the phone wanting to get rid of it.

He was glad that it got his mom off his mind yet at the same time he wasn't because the phone call was already stuck in his head.

I'm watching you. I'm watching you... The voice was stuck in his head and he couldn't get it out. It sounded like there was a high pitch screeching sound in his ear that wouldn't leave. He tried calling David but the phone line was busy. After what seemed like forever he called him again. This time he answered at the fifth ring.

"Who is this?" Was the first thing that he said.

"It's just me." When he heard his Sean's voice he breathed in a sigh of relief.

"I thought you were someone else," he laughed.

"You got the same phone call?"

"I got a phone call and I thought maybe it was you. I thought that maybe you were trying to freak me out or something. How do you know I got a phone call?"

"I got a phone call too."

"Yeah. It sounded more like someone trying to freak you out more than someone playing a prank on you." They were both in silence after a while.

"So what are you doing tonight?"

"Nothing. I was going to go out," Sean walked into the kitchen trying to find something to eat. He stressed out on the word. Just by saying that, David knew what he was talking about.

"Yeah well, that's life buddy. You gotta learn how to deal with it, like how I dealt with mine." They were both silent trying to figure out what to say.

"It seems like four years ago when we first met."

"Yeah. The long silence. Barely even saying a word." They both laughed which was also followed by silence.

"So what do you plan on doing when we get there?"

"I'm going to sit on my ass all day, watch TV, pig out, and listen to some music," Sean grabbed something from the refrigerator and put it on the shelf. He bent down and reached in for a bottle and cracked it open with one hand and took a long gulp.

"That's it. You're not going to go out and have fun or anything?"

"Na. I'd rather just sit and pretty much do nothing. I have enough fun when she's either gone or at home. I make it useful by ignoring that she's gone or at home. That's what I call fun," Sean laughed a little.

"Yeah that's how the days went with mom. If she's home and your gone, know that there's a chance that there's someone there. And if you come home without her not knowing and you go in her room you will be on the floor with blood down your face," David agreed. There was silence once again.

"What are you going to do when we get there?" Sean put a smile on his face.

"Unlike you, I'm going to have fun."

"What kind of fun?" He winked.

"You're sick."

"What?" "You're sick."

"How am I sick?"

"You just are. What are doing?"

"Not much. There's not much to do."

"Yeah." There was a moment of silence between them.

Just then Sean heard someone knocking at his door. He left them knocking until they left which was followed by laughter. He left the kitchen and moved toward the window and watched two kids staring at him and laughing at him.

"Who was that?" David finally asked.

"Just some kids playing around. I hate that. They come here every night to find ways to annoy me. They throw rocks at my window. They ring the doorbell when mom's not home. They just…… ugh. They get on my nerves." David laughed at him.

"Yeah. You get used to for a while."

"Yeah well I'm hoping that I could forget all this when I figure a way out of this hell hole that mom calls home."

"Good luck with that. I hope you find a place and mom doesn't find out."

"Yeah I'll be in big trouble if mom ever found out; she'll rip every part of me to pieces." They both laughed.

"Have you ever gone hiking before?" David tried changing the subject.

"No."

"It's the best I went just a couple weeks ago. Wow. So amazing man. You have to try it out."

"One day when we're all together like a happy family. Not," Sean and David laughed. Just then a knock interrupted their talk. Sean ignored it. He knew it was the kids trying to bug him again. When he heard a low gruff noise he knew it was the cops.

"I know you're in their open the door. We're the cops."

"I gotta go man. There's someone at the door."

"Is it the kids again?"

"No, it's the cops." They both had the same thing in mind.

"I'll see ya later dude." They both hung up. When Sean reached the door, he found his mom stumbling and wavering back and forth.

"We seem to have a situation every night. I'm hoping this doesn't happen again."

"Why don't you both come on in? I'll make you coffee. You look like you both had a rough day," his mom interrupted them with a grin on her face.

"I think you had enough don't you think?" Sean glared at his mom.

"No. It's you who hasn't gotten enough from me," his mom winked at him.

"You're disgusting."

Sean had a disgusting look on his face. She stood in the doorway wavering back and forth.

"Get in there."

She wouldn't go in the house so Sean had to push her in and he went outside closing the door halfway talking with the cops. He could hear his mom making weird noises and he tried to ignore it.

"How long has this been going on for?" Sean asked them after a moment of silence. They heard her making strange noises in the house.

"Is she going to be okay?"

"Oh yeah. She bounces right back up in the morning and gets drunk with her boyfriends." They both raised their eyebrows.

"How long has this actually happened before I was here?" Sean tried to put a little emphasis.

"Do you really want to know?" One of them answered. Sean nodded his head.

"I'm going to have to find out sooner or later."

"This has been going on for over fifteen years. If she doesn't smarten up we have to take her in." Sean folded his head in his hands. He swore under his breath and didn't know what to do.

"Sean," he heard his mom scream from inside.

"I don't know what I'm going to do. I don't know what to do," Sean was on the verge of going crazy.

"Where's David?" One of them asked. Sean looked up with a look that made him think that he said the wrong thing.

"I was just wondering…."

"I know. It's been a while that's all." The other cop interrupted them. Sean just smiled.

"He's doing okay. I'm just glad that he's not here right now or else something crazy would've happened." They all smiled and laughed at the small joke.

"If anything goes wrong or something happens, just let us know. We won't allow this and we won't let this happen again." One of the cops nodded at the door with half a smile on his face.

"Thanks. Oh and uh one more thing. I won't be here for a couple of weeks 'cause I'm going on a trip. So if you'll just let me know when she has to go in or anything," Sean replied after a while.

"Yeah. Don't worry about it. We'll let you know for sure."

"Thank you." They both nodded and left with a smile.

"What do you think he'll say when his mom has to be taken into custody tomorrow, should we tell him?" One of them replied when they were both away from the house.

"No. There's no use anyway. He's well into taking care of himself and needs to adjust in a better environment for now. We'll have to write him a letter or something." It was silent for a while and noise could be heard from their house.

"Why do you always have to embarrass me huh? You could get yourself killed one day," Sean stormed back in the house and locked the door behind him. He moved to the windows and shut the blinds. He didn't want anybody to see them. The neighborhood pretty much knew what was going on by their screams and shouts.

"Come here I want to tell you something."

"No. Get away from me."

"Come here Sean. Let me make you feel better," She added with a grin on her face and a wink. She grabbed his arm. Sean shrugged her hand away.

"Don't touch me. I can hardly believe you ever touched me when I was a baby anyways. I can hardly believe that you even fuckin' loved me," he screamed at his mom. It was enough to bring her back to reality.

"You think I never loved you? I loved you more than I loved David. How can you say I didn't love you huh?"

"Because of the secrets that you kept from me and the things that you said and did to me only to get out of your way. I never thought that it would ever be this way. I always told you that I loved you, but you never even acknowledged it at all." Sean stomped away from her and went to his room and tried to sleep.

He left her lying on the floor by the couch moaning and groaning. Sean kept hearing noise from her. He heard her run to the bathroom and throw up. He tried plugging his ears and tried to think of something else. He wanted to get his mom off his mind for now. There was nothing that seemed right that night and there was nothing that was ever going to make things right. Not even for Sean.

Tracy sat in the den with her brother with a tired look on her face. She didn't know how long she was staring at the wall in front of her lost in a trance, until her brother poked her in the arm.

"Are you okay?" he asked.

"Yeah. I'm fine," she voiced.

"Are you sure?"

"Yeah. I'll be fine," she muttered trying to hide the shakiness in her voice. She left the den and went to her room. Since there wasn't that much to do, Tracy decided to call David.

"Hey what's up, I've been waiting for you to call," he sounded pretty perked up.

"Why don't you come over, I need some company." She fingered her bare neck shaking a bit.

"You know I'm more than that. I'll be there in a bit" She could picture him smiling. When he said that, it brought a smile to her face and some of the things that were on her mind left. She found herself occupied with something that she didn't realize that he came until she overheard her brother talking to him. She made it useful by making noise so that she couldn't hear them talking.

"Hey man, long time no see," her brother replied.

"I know hey?"

"What have you been up to lately?" he smiled with a wink.

"Not much really. Just catching up with work that's all."

"Are you sure about that?" They both laughed.

"I'm sure," David shook his head and smiled.

"Anyways, I uh, gotta go. I have to go to work."

"This late?"

"I know. I'll see ya later. And don't try to do anything that I wouldn't do." He winked. They both laughed as Tracy's brother walked out the door. As he left, David ran the rest of the way upstairs to Tracy's room.

"Hey what's up?" he replied with a smile.

"Not much," she smiled at him.

"You want to tell me why you wanted me to come over?" He slipped onto her bed.

"I told you I need company." She moved closer to him.

"Oh please. You know I'm more than that," he kissed her.

"You know what we should do?" He slipped closer to her and brought his hand to her face. While his other hand slipped between their bodies.

"What?"

"We should order some pizza, make popcorn and watch a movie and see what happens after that. How does that sound?" he brushed her hair back and stared deep into her eyes.

"I like that."

"I know you do." He laughed.

"Come on." She had a smile on her face that made her eyes sparkle. He leaned towards her and kissed her. His lips lingered on hers for more than a while. What they didn't know, what the sparkles in her eyes actually meant.

CHAPTER 4

Josh and Billy were the only ones at home. Josh's suit was crumpled as he sat on top of it on his bed. Billy came into his room without knocking.

"Knock much?" Josh mumbled.

"You're still sitting there?" Billy asked in surprised. Josh ignored Billy and pretended he didn't hear him.

"Leave me alone man. I got my own problems," he groaned.

"Do you even want to go?" Billy asked. Josh just ignored him and turned around and faced the wall. Billy just watched him.

"Suit yourself." Billy turned and left, leaving Josh lying flat on his suit.

He didn't know what college to choose. He walked over towards his desk and went through all the applications in his desk. He was accepted at a few university's he just didn't know which one to choose. He wanted his parent's opinions but he didn't even tell them about any of the applications. He decided it best that it wouldn't do him any good if he lingered on about any of it for a while. He took his heavy sweater and left his room.

He didn't know exactly where he was going. He wandered off and lost track. Time went by and he didn't seem to care at all. He walked recklessly without keeping track or knowing where he was going. He took out a small brown bag from his bulky sweater and took a short drink from it. He was glad that his parents didn't keep track of everything or anything. He took another drink, this time it was a longer heavy drink. It tasted so good. To Josh, it was like swimming in freezing cold water in the summer.

He quickly shoved the bag back into his heavy sweater when he heard two people behind him talking which he thought sounded like teenagers.

"What are you doing out here so late?" one of the guys asked him as he reached Josh. Apparently they weren't teenagers. They were both older, one of which looked heavy built. And the other looked scrawny.

"I'm just trying to clear my mind that's all," Josh explained in little detail.

"Ya sure 'bout that?" the other guy staggered clumsy beside them.

"Cut the crap man," the guy said to the other who was on the other side of Josh. Josh could smell the deep stench of scotch and whiskey on the guy's clothes and breaths.

"What? I'm just trying to have fun," he looked like was about to go in a coma.

"Will you be fine?"

"Yeah. Thanks." They both walked off with the other guy still laughing and couldn't stop.

"I'm just trying to have fun. I'm just trying to have fun," he kept repeating until the other guy slapped him hard on the back. The guy fell hard on the ground still conscious. He laughed as he fell hard.

"Come on man. Quit foolin' around." He helped him up. Just as he got up, he ran. The other guy ran after him. Josh watched them chase after each other until they rounded the corner and lost themselves in the midst.

He took out the bag from his sweater and gave it one last swig. He stared at the corner where the two guys left for a while until he got tired. Before he turned around to leave, he thought he saw Sean for a second. He squinted his eyes to see if he saw right. He thought he saw Sean with a bloody knife in his hand. He shook his head, knowing that the drink was making him see things. He took one last quick glance and left.

Sean stood there still. He watched Josh walk away after a brief hesitation. With a knife in his hand, he licked it clean from the ketchup with a paper towel. He walked back inside to finish making a sandwich. He knew that he wasn't going to be able to sleep anyways. He watched his mom slumped up against the couch and went back to the kitchen.

When Josh got home, he still couldn't get that vivid image of Sean holding a bloody knife and smiling. What if it wasn't blood? What if it was something else? Maybe he was smiling because he saw me as a way to say hi. But how could he see that far? Josh shook those thoughts away. He just wanted to go to his room and sleep.

If only I didn't leave the house none of that would have ever happened. His mind was ramming with thoughts that he never experienced before. He tried warming up milk for him to calm down. He burned his lips and cursed under his breath. He skipped the glass and dumped the milk down the sink. He didn't know what else to do.

Finally, he decided to go to bed after ten minutes, which was only making things worse because he was the only one home and it was dead silent in the house. He wished that he went with Billy, but something made him say no.

Upstairs in his room, he tried to relax. In the far distance he could hear the wail of a siren going off. He heard it pass the neighbor's house and stop. He tried ignoring it by turning around from the window and tried to sleep. Josh heard the doorbell ring a couple times. He thought that it was just his friends trying to bug him. The doorbell rang again and this time it got on his nerves. He went downstairs to get rid of who it was that was ringing the doorbell like a lunatic. He opened the door to get rid of them.

"Look man, I…" he stopped in midsentence. He was shocked to see that it wasn't his friends. It was the cops.

"We're here because two cops were killed. We're going around a couple of the neighborhood to see if anyone knows," one cop replied getting right to the situation. The cop glowered and interrupted the silence.

"No sorry, I don't know anything", Josh tried ignoring them, but the other guy caught him first.

"I'm sure you do. Because a neighbor told us you were watching them a couple blocks down."

"What do you want from me? I didn't kill those cops," he shrilled. He wasn't sure if they were talking about the two guys that he saw. If they were talking about them, he didn't even know that they were cops. He thought that they were a bunch of guys high on something.

"I'm not saying that. I…"

"None of those neighbors down there don't know who I am. And now you're here to accuse me of something that I didn't do because of one stupid neighbor?" Josh was wide awake now. He was glad that nobody was home and that he was the only one.

"We're not accusing you," Randy stopped the fight between Josh and the other cop before it got worse and someone got hurt.

"Then what are you trying to do?"

"Let's just settle this the right way. Why don't the three of us go inside before we get bitten," he finally got some of it settled.

When they were inside, Josh made them coffee as Randy suggested. Josh tried explaining to them both what happened. He excluded his friend out of it. He didn't want Sean to get in trouble for something that he didn't entirely do. One of the cops tried getting everything written, while the other cops just stared at him not sure whether to believe what he was saying.

"Is there anything else?"

"No."

"Mind if we look around your house for some evidence?" he gave them permission to look around. The other cop followed with him still staring at Josh. Josh sat on the couch with his head in hands as they searched the house. He couldn't believe what stupid idiot would put him in a situation like this. He wanted to run right then.

"Well, there seems to be nothing here," the same guy that was giving him a hard time walked in. He walked up to Josh who was still sitting on the couch rubbing his head.

"Listen to me and listen to me clearly. I don't like fights and I don't intend to get in a fight with you. I want you to understand what I'm telling you. Got it?" A nod was all he wanted from him and a nod was all he got. The cop quickly left outside before anything happened. Josh sat there quietly waiting for the other cop to come out.

"Well there seems to be nothing here, so you'll be fine. Listen uh, if anyone says anything or says something happens, call me," he replied lowering his voice as he gave Josh a card.

"Does that include a cop harassing you when you didn't do anything and blames you for no reason?" Josh gasped.

"Don't worry about it. To tell you the truth, he's still in training. So if anything like that happens with him or anyone else, just give me a call," Randy replied with a smile.

"Now why don't you try to forget that all this happened, and put it to sleep? You don't want your friends to see you troubled." He gave Josh a pat on the back and left.

When he said that, he thought of Sean. He walked towards the window and watched the car leave. He heard the wailing of the siren go off in the night. He thought he saw one of the cops stare at him. Josh shook his head and backed away from the window and breathed in a sigh of relief. He wasn't sure if he was able to sleep at all.

CHAPTER 5

Everything seemed very quiet that morning. Sean walked downstairs to the kitchen to find something to eat. He turned to the refrigerator to find a note. He didn't bother to read it. He just gave it a quick glance and threw it on the shelf. He knew that his mother would do anything crazy to get things off her mind. She doesn't even ask me what I want, she doesn't even care. Hell, she barely even knows that I exist; he slammed the refrigerator door hard and went back to his room.

He tried taking things off his mind. He tried taking his mom off of his mind. He walked into her room to find everything gone. He went through her drawers and her closet even in her bathroom, everything was gone. He ran back downstairs to read the note that his mom left.

'Dear Sean, I don't know how to say this, but I'm leaving. I always wanted you to have a better life and I didn't want you to turn into me or any of the men I have met. I'm sorry. I'm leaving for now to try and live on my own for now. I hope you understand why I left. I'm trying the best I can to change myself. I love you.'

He just shook his head in disbelief. Why would she do this to me? He muttered a curse under his breath repeatedly. He tried to think of something else but he couldn't. He cried for his mom, he cried for his dad (if he even knew he had a dad). He just cried not knowing what to do. He was occupied with what he was thinking and what might happen to him that he didn't hear the phone ring. At the fifth ring he finally picked up.

"Hey Sean. Are you ready or what?"

"Yeah," he muttered slowly and quietly that he wasn't sure that David heard him. He barely had a grip on the phone so it slid from his fingers but he quickly caught it.

"You okay buddy?"

"Yeah. Yeah. I'm fine," he cleared his throat and talked a little louder.

"You sure? We don't want you to feel empty on a nice warm day like this," David replied with laughter. Sean looked out the window and saw a few clouds hovering in the sky. It seemed more of a gloomy day to him rather than a warm day.

"I'm fine."

"Sure you are. Anyways I'll see ya later." They both hung up. Sean stood there by the phone waiting for his mom call, but she never. Even after all the days that he told her that him and his friends were going on a trip she didn't even bother to call.

The day rolled by quickly and as fast as possible to get it over and done with. When the evening all came for them, they were psyched. They all met at David's house. They all had a great time, except for Sean. Sarah and Heather took a quick glance at him and didn't even bother to talk to him. Sean overheard Billy talking to Heather.

"Why do you spend more of your time with Sarah?"

"Because she wants me to."

"Well why don't you start talking to Tracy so she feels good about something for once?"

"Sarah will get mad at me if I talk to her."

"Well then you're making the biggest mistake of your life. Tracy needs you more than Sarah and I don't give a damn about her even though she's my girlfriend." Billy turned and walked away when he saw Sarah coming towards them.

"What was that all about?" Sarah glared at her.

"Nothing. He was just being nice that's all," Heather hid the guilt in her eyes. She felt the guilt leave her when she saw Sarah roll her eyes.

"Do you want to leave? I'm kinda getting tired of this."

"No. I want to stay. You can go if you want,"

"Suit yourself," Sarah scoffed and left. Now that Sarah was gone, Heather moved toward the kitchen and sat with Tracy and talked happily.

"What's the matter with you?" Billy looked at Sean.

"Nothing. Nothing," he muttered under his breath not caring if he heard him or not. He sulked in the corner and didn't want to be bothered. He just wished that he could turn things around and make it better, but he knew that he couldn't do that.

"Come on Sean. Everybody's having fun except for you," David came in.

"I'm not in the mood to have any fun right now." David moved and sat beside him.

"Tell me what's wrong."

"I told you nothing's wrong," he spread his hands out in exasperation.

"I know there's something wrong. I wanna know." Sean leaned back against the wall and hit his head hard against the wall.

"Is it mom?"

"Yeah," he stared at the floor. There was a long moment of silence between them.

"Would you let me move in with you? I mean like get the hell away from that house and stay with you since you have no life compared to mine."

"Why?"

"I just wanna get the hell out of that house."

"Mom needs you and you're just gonna leave her?"

"Mom doesn't need me. She has her damn boyfriends to keep her satisfied. Did I tell you what she did?" David just shook his head. Sean moved away from the wall and stared at him.

"She took all her stuff and left. She left some stupid note saying that it was best for her if she just leaves." David's eyes went wide in shock.

"You didn't see the note or anything this morning?" David just shook his head.

"Are you just saying that or did she actually leave?"

"She left. All her clothes ....everything.... it's all gone," Sean was mad at himself. They both sat there quietly thinking about it.

"You know what I still don't feel sorry for her after all the things she did to us."

"Don't say that. She needs us and we need her."

"Yeah right."

"It's nobody's fault."

"Yeah well what about you?"

"What about me?"

"You left as soon as you could without telling me."

"I didn't leave."

"Really?" David sighed and told him everything.

"One day while you were still at work, I went to see mom. I went and found her all wrapped in her bed and there was someone else there but I couldn't see. I left the room and mom came after me and she yelled at me just for barging in on her like that. She said. "Don't you dare come in my room like that. You know better than me not to do that." I said sorry but she didn't buy it. Then we got into a huge fight and I saw these two guys walking downstairs and I knew right off the bat who they were. Instead of fighting with mom the whole entire time. I went and fought with them both. They were both crying on the floor like babies. Mom yelled at me for that. We got into a huge fight and mom slapped me and pushed me down the stairs and told me to leave and never come back.

"That was the last time I saw mom. Before I left I saw her sitting by the window crying and she didn't even bother to say she was sorry and she didn't even bother to watch me leave," David finished off his sentence with a long swig of the bottle. Sean stared at him in amazement.

"So technically she kicked you out?" He nodded without a shrug.

"Where did you get the money for the house and everything?"

"I stole it."

"What?"

"Yup. Mom doesn't even have a damn clue," he nodded.

"Did mom tell you anything about going anywhere or where she was going?"

"No. She just wrote a note. Didn't even bother to say where she was going. Why? What's going on?" Sean wanted to know what was going on or what might have happened.

"Nothing."

"Tell me." David drew in a heavy sigh.

"Remember when I tell you you're going to be very mad."

"I don't care."

"You're going to make me regret it."

"I seriously don't care. I want to know. What's going on?"

"You're going to kill me after I tell you."

"I don't care. Just tell me before I kill you anyways."

"Mom might go to jail because of the way she constantly drinks every night and does all that crap. I think she just wrote the note to tell you that she did leave but they might've taken her in for custody." Sean's face grew pale. He wanted to scream. He wanted to throw something against the wall.

"I told you. I knew it wasn't a good idea." David saw the look on his face.

"Why? I mean why did she tell you, but not me?"

"I have no idea."

"There has to be a reason why she told you and not me."

"I don't know. Probably because she knows one of us will handle it better."

"How did you handle it when she told you?"

"Let's just not talk about this for now. I'm sick and tired of talking about this crap." David got up and walked to the kitchen. Sean watched him wrap his arms around Tracy and smiled leaving all the pain behind. Sean was shocked how David just let it all pass. He never seemed to linger on one thing. He always made a way to get rid of the pain and it never showed, not even in front of him or anybody. Sean just sighed and sat there for a really long time.

The evening drew faster than the morning. They were all excited about the next day and their plans for the trip. Tracy and Heather sat in the kitchen exchanging thoughts and ideas about what they were going to get and what they were going to do.

Josh and Billy also sat in the kitchen and were in a heated discussion about the presidential debate and what they thought of the new president of the United States. David and Sean sat in the den talking and thinking aloud about what they were going to do and what they thought was going to happen. Tracy, Heather, Josh, and Billy all moved towards the den wondering what David and Sean were up to.

"Their probably setting a mood," Josh and Billy laughed.

"You're not funny you know that," Heather looked at him.

"You always used to think I'm funny what happened to that huh?"

"That was after you started acting weird." Both Heather and Tracy laughed.

"The only person is weird here is you."

"I don't think so."

"Really? What makes you think you're better than me?" He moved towards her and was about to wrap his arms around her.

"I'm not saying that I'm better than you." She turned around to face him.

"Then what exactly are you saying?" He smiled an evil grin. She turned around and left. She caught up with Tracy and raced downstairs to the basement. Josh followed them and ran after them and Billy walked toward the den.

"What are you guys doing?"

"Nothing much. We're just talking about the same old things." Their conversation was erupted with laughter and screams. They all got up to see what was going on. They ran to the basement to find Heather and Tracy wet from the pool.

"What's going on? Why are you all wet" David asked in amazement as he saw them dripping wet as they walked towards them.

"Josh pushed us in the pool and we had to push him back." Tracy and Heather laughed. Behind them, Josh walked with a limp and was dripping wet.

"That wasn't funny you know."

"It was to me."

"Who's wants to help me with payback?" No one replied. David walked silently behind Tracy and carried her back to the pool.

"I will." Tracy screamed with laughter as he drove her back to the pool. Sean ended up carrying Heather to the pool who also screamed with laughter. They all ended up in the pool wet and exhausted. They all blew in a sigh of relief, happy that they were all having fun for the first time.

"Too bad Sarah wasn't here," Josh replied with a grin on his face.

"Who cares," Heather replied back and pushed him in the water.

"I will never forgive you for that," Josh gasped for air as he came back up.

"I'm not asking you to." They all cried with laughter that hung in the air. They didn't know exactly what the time was. They got out of the pool splashing each other as they got out. As Josh was getting out of the pool, Heather pushed him back in. They laughed at him as he sputtered water out of his mouth.

"I think you made him mad," Billy laughed. Heather watched him get out of the pool and run after her.

He grabbed her and threw her in the pool. He jumped back in the pool at the same time.

"At least we're even now."

"Yeah that's all you think about anyways." They both laughed. Josh kissed her softly on the lips. They both got out of the pool and walked into the den where the rest of them were. They walked to the living room in the basement and relaxed for a while. There was a moment of silence in the air between the six of them.

"What makes you all think that we should drive rather than going in a plane tomorrow?" Billy asked them.

"What?" Sean laughed. They all laughed at Billy because of what he said. He had to laugh himself.

"No. I'm saying that when we go tomorrow, should we take a plane or should we drive?"

"Plane." Both Tracy and Heather screamed and laughed when they said it at the same time.

"Jinx. You owe me a soda." They both said it at the same time and laughed.

"What do you think?" He nodded his head towards David and Sean and Josh.

"Doesn't really matter."

"It does make a difference actually. Because when you drive it will probably take more than twenty- four hours to get there. That includes how long you drive at night the stops that we make. Whereas in a plane, well you all know where I'm going with this," Sean explained. They all stared at him.

"What?"

"Nothing. We just thought that maybe you happened to be an expert or something like that," Josh laughed hard.

"I am actually. And if anyone has a problem with that speak up or forever hold your peace." No one said anything.

"That's what I thought."

"Does anybody have any suggestions about Sean 'cause I do," Heather replied. They all laughed.

"What time is it?" Josh answered.

"What you wanna go to bed already?"

"No. I just want to know so we don't look out to find the sun in the sky."

"My phone says it's twelve. I put it an hour ahead," David replied.

"My phone says it's twelve too. I don't know dude. Why don't you go check the clock upstairs we changed ours an hour ahead for the trip." Josh walked upstairs to find the time. When he was gone, David busted out laughing.

"What?"

"I don't have a clock." They all laughed at Josh when he came back downstairs.

"You find the time?"

"No. Oh well I'll figure it out later." They were all lost in the time that they didn't exactly know what time it was. Josh was the first one to sleep. They stared at Josh and kept poking at him but he wouldn't wake up. Staring at Josh, made them all tired.

One by one, they all got tired and weary looking. Soon enough they were all fast asleep. They couldn't wait till the dawn broke out and the fun that they were going to have. The only thing that they could think of was the fun that they were going to have. They thought of nothing else.

CHAPTER 6

Wen dawn broke out, they all looked tired and beat. They didn't want to wake up early that morning; they just wanted to sleep more. Some of them were just plain grumpy. David who was already up before any of them, tried waking them up. He tried pulling them off the blankets they were sleeping on. He ignored their cries when they mumbled aloud. Tracy woke up next and took his hand in hers. He took her hand and kissed her cheek. They both smiled at each other. "Morning Beautiful."

"Morning. I'm going to go home for a bit if that's okay," she told him.

"Sure. I'll wait for you." He smiled at her before she left.

They were all peevish and were exhausted from last night. Billy woke up next from his goodnight's rest and wiped away all the drowsiness from his eyes. He walked into the kitchen where David was.

"Where's Tracy?" He added with a wink. David pushed him against the wall when he did that.

"She just went home. She had to do something. So what do you think?" David replied after a long moment of silence.

"Not bad. I think Josh passed out before we did. And there's a good chance if he doesn't woke up before Sean." They both laughed.

"What are guys talking 'bout?" Sean stumbled in the kitchen and went to the refrigerator to look for something to eat.

"Nothing much. Just talking about last night. That's pretty much it." They watched Sean pop out a bottle and take a quick long swig.

Both David and Billy looked at each other. They shook their heads at Sean. Sean took another drink. This time he just let it all go.

"A little thirsty there aren't you Sean?" David asked him. Sean dipped the last gulp in his mouth.

"Shut up. At least I have a reason why I'm drinking early in the morning," he glared at the two full bottles on the shelf in front of them and walked off.

"What's his problem?" Billy wondered aloud. David just shrugged. He didn't want him to know about anything that they talked about last night. The day dragged by. Everyone else was up except for Josh just as they all expected.

"Is he ever like this?" Sean wondered.

"I have no idea. All I know is that he sleeps good when he drinks. Half the time I don't know what he does and he sleeps like a baby," Billy sorted it out for them.

"Huh." They ignored Josh and tried to find something else to do. It got bored for them so they tried poking Josh for fun to get him to wake up.

"Who ever is doing that I'm gonna kill you," Josh mumbled in his sleep. They laughed at him and waited for him to wake up. They thought that he was awake but he was nowhere being awake.

"Does he ever talk in his sleep?" Sean asked.

"Sometimes. The other times I don't know what he does in his sleep. One time I caught him sleepwalking. He was walking downstairs and we had company and they wouldn't leave. So he came walking downstairs talking to himself. They all thought he was on something. I laughed so hard." Billy was laughing.

"I have an idea," David smiled. They each took a side and a part of Josh and carried him downstairs. They went down one more staircase and one more door. There, they threw him in the pool. They all had a good laugh. When he got out of the pool, he flaunted them with water.

"Hey, these are my favorite plaid pants," Sean cried.

"Like I care. And that was not funny," Josh mumbled through sleep and drew out water from his ears. He left them standing there watching him and still laughing at him.

When the hour came for their departure, they were glad that they were leaving. They were still a bit exhausted but they managed through the rest of the morning. Their attitudes changed that morning to being anxious which got them ready to leave.

"Thank god we're leaving. I just wish we were already there," Sean's voice exhausted everyone.

"Will you quit complaining? It's getting on my nerves," Josh drew a heavy sigh.

"You're getting on my nerves."

"You're all getting on our nerves." David, Tracy and Billy shouted at them at the same time. They all laughed.

They finally left wanting to get on the highway as fast as they can, but the traffic was moving slow. They thought that leaving early would get them on the highway quicker. Instead, they left later that morning and the traffic was prolonged than ever. They waited about an hour and a half for the traffic to start moving.

Even though the traffic was slow, there was no accident to cause such a delay. Cars were honking, other were shouting, and the roads got intense from the heat ignition and caused a great big commotion. Josh leaped out of the car to see what was going on. Reaching the front, he saw four cars blocking the lane in deep full conversation. They looked like as if they were there all night. One of the guys on the car turned to him.

"Yes? You got a problem?" the guy answered.

"Actually I do. Either you start moving while the light is still green, or I call the cops and we can discuss what you ladies have to say," Josh snapped open his cell phone and angered his voice even more. He moved back when they started their cars and left. One of the guys mumbled a curse under his breath but Josh didn't catch what it was he said. A couple of cars were able to go before the light turned red. He jumped back into the car and smiled at himself.

"What was that all about?" Billy wondered aloud.

"Just some guys talking like they're on a prime time show. But they weren't cracking any jokes," Josh added with laughter. Sean and

David joined in with him. The traffic eagerly dispersed into different directions.

They were all sober for quite a while. Five minutes later, the stereo blared in the car. Other cars passed by and stared at them with looks on their faces.

"This music sounds so lame. What the hell is it anyway?" Josh piped up.

"It's called shut the hell up and be quiet by me," Billy laughed. Josh openly mocked his laughter.

"Oh you're so funny."

"I know I am." Josh just stared at him and shook his head.

"Why not play this kind?" Sean brought in. He reached through the back to the front and put in a cd. The stereo was loud and upbeat with music.

"Now that's what I call music. Westlife music," Sean beamed.

"If you want another cd, I got more."

"How much do you have with you right now?" Josh looked at him in bewilderment.

"Well not thinking about it, I have what, some of their albums." Sean turned in his seat to face him.

"Why you got a problem with that?"

"No not really."

"Just because I packed more than a week of clothing and a lot of cd's, which mostly are all Westlife. Well, some aren't. Anyways, what does that even matter to you Dumbo?" Sean took in a breath after that.

"Never mind. My fault for asking."

"You bet it was." There was a long heated conversation between Sean and Josh. Another heated discussion went towards Sarah and Heather about what they thought about the trip and what they were going to get when they get to Darwin. Billy sat there in the front quietly driving with no one bothering him. He smiled to himself; he didn't really like anybody bothering him when he was driving. Billy managed a conversation with Tracy.

"What do you think so far of the trip so far?" he asked.

"Not bad. If it's worth driving all day and night in here when it's cramped with a bunch of us, then I think it's fun. All though my suggestion about going on a plane was much better," Tracy smiled. Billy smiled back. David, who sat beside Tracy, seemed quiet throughout the ride.

He never really found anything to say. He felt deserted even though the car was crammed with all of them. David scrunched himself in the corner. He felt Tracy's hands on his. He lifted his head and smiled at her. They both smiled at each other and stared into each other's eyes for a while.

"Look like's someone is getting a little comfy back there," Sarah replied with heat in her voice.

"I can't believe that you didn't tell us that you and David are together," Sarah demanded towards Tracy. She just ignored her and tried to think of something else.

"Everybody knows except for you. You're the only one that thinks that everything revolves around you when it revolves around more than one person," Sean answered breaking the tension and the silence.

"Wow. And we thought that you were dumb," Billy replied.

"Who said I was dumb?" Billy made a face at Sean. David and Tracy turned toward the window and

David wrapped his arms around her.

"You know what I was thinking about a couple of nights ago?" David turned to her.

"What?" Tracy smiled.

"I was thinking about your birthday and last night and how much fun I had."

"I was thinking of the same thing. And I'm still thinking about it now." They smiled at each other and David leaned in closer and kissed her. His lips lingered on hers for a while.

"I love you so much you know that?" He traced his fingers in her hair.

"Yes I do. And I love you too." They both smiled and laughed.

"When was the last time you cut your hair? It's beautiful." He ran his hand through her silky brown hair.

"The last time you told me not to."

"When was that?"

"A really long time ago." They both smiled at each other once again.

The stereo that was on full blast was shut off. It was quiet between them for a while. Cars passed by with teenagers screaming and howling, glad that high school was out for them and they were able to go somewhere by themselves for a couple of weeks or maybe a couple of months before school started again for them. It wasn't like that for any of them.

They finished high school a while back and now they are going to university. Things went by fast for them. Billy zoned in and out of reality. His mind was in different worlds from his friends. He was too occupied with what he was thinking that he didn't realize a bottle hit the back of his car and probably made a dent. He also didn't realize that there was a car beside them trying to keep the same pace with him.

"Nice car," the driver replied. Billy pretended he didn't hear him. He ignored him and went a bit faster. The other car sped up with his.

"What's wrong Billy? Aren't you guilty of anything yet?" he whooped out with laughter and his friends trailed along. Billy was getting frustrated and annoyed. He drove faster to get rid of the car. He knew exactly who that was. He just didn't want to get in another fight with him like he did in high school.

Billy knew that he was bad luck and a bad seed. The car sped up with his and played around with him until he relented from Billy's attitude. Billy drove a lot faster and lost the other car in the midst. He finally slowed down when he saw a police car drive by.

"You'll be sorry," he shouted as he drove off and threw another bottle at his car. Billy swerved his car and the bottle missed. The other car drove faster to get rid of Billy's car, he just knew that he wasn't going to get rid of his face in his head. The police car turned its siren on and went after the car.

The car didn't stop until another police car came. He finally pulled off onto the side of the road. Billy passed by and didn't slow down. He thought he saw him give him the finger, but he didn't seem to care at all.

Soon enough, they were all tired. They were tired from the excitement that happened and they were tired from the excitement that was going to happen next. Billy drove for a while until he found a motel in the middle of where they were going to get their rest. They found themselves a room, and quickly adjusted to it. Some of them got their own room because they couldn't handle much of anyone else when they complained. In less than ten minutes, they all fell asleep.

CHAPTER 7

They all woke up early in the morning ready to leave. Josh woke up grumpy because he never slept well that night. None of them slept well that night. Billy had nightmares of that guy and still couldn't get him out of his head. They just wanted to finish the rest of the trip to Darwin and go back home and relax. David slipped his arms around Tracy and watched the sun rise. Tracy felt the eye of Sarah on her. She quickly turned her gaze from Sarah and tried to look on the bright side of things, which was hard for her to do because of Sarah.

They were all tired and weary, but they didn't seem to show it. Once again, Billy drove with Sarah in the front and the others in the back, switching seats from time to time. David reached under the seat and grabbed a bottle. Sean stared at him.

"What?"

"You gonna hog all the damn bottles?" David reached under the seat for two bottles and gave one to Sean and Josh.

"That's better," Sean replied and took a long swig. David stared at him with a smile on his face and watched him chug it down his mouth and reached for another.

"What?"

"Nothing." Sarah turned and gazed at them through the mirror.

"You got a problem?" Sean staggered.

"How about drinking water for starters?" Sarah pushed.

"Tried. Doesn't work for me."

"You wanna pass me one?" Billy turned his arm for one while he drove with one hand. David was about to reach a bottle for him, but Sarah stopped him.

"I don't think it's a good idea," Sarah glowered.

"Why not?" Billy almost shrieked.

"Remember what happened at Michelle's birthday party after we left?"

"Good times. Good times," Sean smiled and turned to Josh who laughed. They were all drunk that night. Billy was drunk more than his friends were. He kept making jokes and laughing for no reason and staggered to the car. When he started the car, he didn't realize that it was on reverse, and he drove right into a tree.

"Remember that time when you were drunk and you were trying to back out of the driveway and you drove all the way back and hit the neighbor's car?" Josh laughed hysterically and stared at Sarah. David, Billy, and Sean joined in.

"Or how 'bout the time when Sarah almost got out of a ticket from a cop when she was flirting with him?" Sean brought in.

"Please stop," Sarah turned to the window wanting the conversation to end.

"I don't know why I even brought that up," Sarah sighed while the rest of them laughed.

"Oh come on Sarah have a little fun. We're just joking around. Besides it was just a one time thing. It's not going to happen again. Trust me," Billy waved his hands in the air with a smile all over his face. His smile faded when Sarah didn't bother to take it all as a joke.

"I don't care. I don't want to take that risk again," Sarah ended the conversation and turned back to the window. Billy kept looking at her from time to time. He wanted to change her mind, yet at the same time she won't let him. He finally drew a heavy sigh and not a word was spoken to each other. Sean and Josh kept glancing at each other waiting for the right moment to laugh and they did. Heather and Tracy talked quietly between each other.

They thought that they saw Sarah give Heather a menacing glare because she was talking to Tracy. They ended their conversation between each other and Tracy moved back beside David and he hugged her close in his arms. They all fell asleep in the car with soft music playing.

The night finally drew near and they were still on the road. One by one, they all caught a cold that lasted for about a couple of hours, and they were each getting on each other's nerves. Billy gripped the steering wheel as his hands began to slip. He drove on until he found a gas station.

Turning off the ignition, he tried to sleep, but couldn't. The gas station was still open on the inside so he decided to go in since he wasn't going to sleep at all. The light was bright, but it dimmed a little. The aisles were so close together that you almost had to squeeze right through them. Everything was strewn around as if someone tried to hurry it up during a burglary.

There was a stale stench in the air that seemed to cling to everything around it. The freezer doors at the end were foggy and unclear. The handles seemed mired to the other side as Billy tried to open one. He tried walking over boxes that were either empty or full with whatever was inside them. It was hot and stuffy and damp inside.

"Can I help you?" someone answered from behind. Billy jumped from the deep voice behind him that startled him. He reeled on his feet to turn around. Besides his deep voice, the guy looked scrawny and big. His facial features were gray and bold with a slight mustache that he gripped with his hand.

His handsome features seemed to fade away as he got older. He fingered his unshaven mustache and beard as if he was thinking something over. His muscles were broad and heavy. His bluish-green eyes sparkled and glimmered in the light. He rocked on his heels like Billy's dad always does. His smile was nothing but a scowl.

"Uh no. I'm fine," Billy finally spoke.

"Are you sure? You look kind of restless," there was something about the guy's voice. He sounds concerning and nice, Billy thought.

"I'm just a bit tired. My friends and I are headed to Darwin."

"That's a long drive from here. How many hours are on you?"

"I'm not sure. None of us are keeping track of time," Billy said, following him to the counter.

"What happened here?" Billy surveyed the rest of the small place.

"My family used to work here. My parents gave it up for some company, but my older brothers took it out of their hands. So now I'm left to take care of it. It's been very messy here lately. I've been robbed twice as you can see, but I happened to manage it all. I was never able to put things out anymore. Who knows I just might get robbed again. Money seems short. I barely have anyone coming in these days." There was tension between them. The only noise that could be heard was the low humming noise of the electricity running.

"So do you need anything?" He replied after a long moment of silence. Billy stood there in a daze. His voice got him back to reality. Billy poured a bunch of snacks, chocolate bars, and a beer for himself on the countertop. He smiled at Billy and at the stuff that he wanted. He smiled back at him and gave him more money than he half expected Billy would give him. Billy left with two bags and a bottle in his hand and the bell rang when he opened the door and left.

Outside, Billy let out a sigh of relief. He smelled the fresh air which was refreshing than the stench inside. He checked his watch and saw the sun peeking out a little from behind the scene in front of him. He turned around when he heard a groan.

"Where are we? Why aren't we moving?" Sarah moaned under her breath.

"Don't worry. Relax. We only stooped for a short bit," Billy replied. Even though he knew that it was more than just a short bit that they stopped for.

"Are we even close? I'm getting tired of this," Sarah whined.

"We're all tired, so quit complaining," Sean uttered in the back seat. Billy finished the rest of the beer and threw it in the trash and quickly got in the car before a fight erupted.

"Who wants to switch spots with me, I'm sick of this spot. I've been sitting in it for hours," Sean complained.

"I will. I need the back anyways," Sarah answered giving Billy a hard glance before she moved. Billy just shook his head. When they switched spots, they made themselves comfortable.

"Now I'm in shot gun. Ha ha," Sean relaxed. Billy watched him sink deep into the seat. It was quiet for a while after they were on the road. Sean put the radio on and switched to the cd that played soft music.

"So Billy what do you think of Josh," Sean brought up conversation in the hot damp car. He stared at him and smiled and waited for him to reply. Billy just ignored him and pretended he didn't hear him.

"What do you think of David?" Billy brought in.

"I think of him as being annoying. He's so loud."

"Like you would know," David came along.

"Tell me that's not loud?"

"You're louder than me. Remember that time we had a screaming contest. You were the loudest. You practically broke every window in the house."

"He's right. You are loud Sean," Josh put in.

"Yeah well, he was just jealous because I won the contest."

"Yeah right. My ears were plugged for weeks because of that."

"Anyways, come on Billy answer my question." Sean turned away from David who made a face at him.

"I don't know. I think he's weird that's all," Billy announced.

"You think I'm weird?" Josh shrilled. All the guys laughed at him. Billy didn't exactly see where he was going because he lost himself in the conversation. Someone was supposed to head him in the right direction but nobody was leading him.

The passing of other cars stopped. Instead of turning left where he was supposed to, he turned right. Soon enough, signs were missing; the once dense trees were beginning to grow scarce. The road that was once smooth gave in to hard gravel.

Billy stopped talking and laughing and his face went pale and was filled with confusion. When they all realized that they weren't on the road, everyone stopped talking all at once and their faces were filled with confusion and fear.

The only noise that Billy could hear was the beating of his heart and his mind screaming in agony and frustration. A hard bump on the road brought their conversation to a halt and brought them back to reality. He stopped for a minute to think things over. In the silence in the back, Billy heard Tracy let out a short gasp.

CHAPTER 8

The guy who held Tracy didn't let go. He dragged his long fingernails around her neck. He let his breath trail along her neck, which brought a chill down her spine, and she shivered.

"Let go of her," David demanded. He knew that yelling at him would do no good. He didn't seem to hear him. David turned to him and shoved him. He brought back a hard slap against David's face and blood poured from his face where he dragged his fingernails. He turned back to Tracy and whispered in her ear.

"I'll be back for you," he growled. Before he left he dragged his tongue in her ear. He pushed her back inside the car. Tracy gasped for breath.

"Are you okay Tracy?" David hugged her close.

"Yeah, I'm fine," she quivered and clung to his embrace. David seemed to forget the slap and the pain the guy gave him. He held her close in his arms not letting her go. There was a moment of silence between them. They still didn't forget what had happened. The image of the guy hurting Tracy kept coming back to him.

"Okay, Where to?" Josh tried pulling in conversation between the thick air that was held for a while between the seven of them.

"What do you mean 'where to'? We're practically in the middle of nowhere," Sarah raised her voice.

"Relax. It's just a joke."

"Well there's not going to be joke when we're lost," Sarah hardened her tone. Everyone turned blunt and the air turned thick between them once again.

Driving around was useless for Billy. They had enough of it all, especially Billy. He was the one who planned the trip and he was the one that wanted to go with his friends trailing behind. Billy drove around for hours trying to get out. The sky above them darkened fast. The stars that once shown its light, were hidden behind dark clouds that threatened them with a storm. Sarah got impatient by the second.

"This is so stupid. This trip was supposed to lead us somewhere not to the middle of nowhere." Billy sighed heavily. No one said a word.

In the backseat, David hugged his arms around Tracy and fell asleep in them. David drew his head against the seat and fell asleep. Sean and Josh made small conversation while Heather slept peacefully in the backseat who had no clue in what was going on. Heather had been sleeping the whole time that she didn't hear Tracy scream.

"This is so stupid," Sean whispered.

"Why did we even bother to come?" Josh agreed.

"It was mostly all Billy's idea for the trip. We're just tagging along for his sake." They both shook their heads at didn't say anything for a while.

"You know what amazed me the most though? The concert," Josh brought up.

"Yeah. That was the best concert ever."

"We all got the best out of it," Sean nodded in agreement. They grew silent once again.

Heather woke up and sat up straight. When she stretched her arms, she punched Sean.

"Ow."

"Sorry." David was the last to wake up ten minutes after he felt Tracy slip away. Tracy fingered the scratch on his face. He winced.

"Does it hurt?"

"A little." The touch of her fingers drew away the pain that he felt. He locked his eyes on hers and they both knew exactly what they were thinking.

"Guess what everybody, we are now officially...." Sarah left her sentence hanging, waiting for someone to finish it off, but no one did. She finished it off herself.

"....screwed." Billy gasped in horror, as he realized that they were driving around in circles. It was midnight and there was not a trace of a star leading them anywhere. There was no reverberation of cars passing by or cars honking at one another. They were stranded in the middle of nowhere.

"Great," Billy groaned.

"Where are we?" Heather shivered trying to adjust to the darkness.

"This doesn't look like the road we were on before," Sarah started to realize.

"You think?" Josh shot back. They were starting to get on each other's nerves and the air between them was getting thicker by the minute. Billy continued on driving in the darkness.

"This is nice," Sarah had a sarcastic tone but no one caught it.

"I swear to god I will hurt you if you don't shut up," Josh yelled.

"Don't tell me to shut up."

"I will if you don't stop talking." Now that they were lost, they thought that arguing will get to them, but it wasn't taking them anywhere.

"Let's just get out and see if we can find a gas station or something," Heather finally suggested as she began to realize what was going on.

"I don't think we can. I think we're lost," Sean revealed. They all huddled close together. The darkness loomed over them trying to give up their hopes of freedom.

CHAPTER 9

"**T**his is nice," Sarah repeated as they were being driven around in circles.

"Just shut up for once. Fuck," Sean cried.

"Why don't all of you shut up? We're stranded in the fuckin' middle of nowhere, and all you can do is fight?" Billy shouted over top everyone else's. He fingered his temples and drew in a heavy sigh.

"All we have to do right now, is to relax and calm down. We might as well stay here for a while," Billy tried relaxing his tone and drew another sigh. It was quiet for a moment until Sean made up his own decision.

"Well you know what, you guys can wait here all the fuck you want, but I had enough. I'm out of here," Sean jumped out of the car and walked off. They all watched Sean disappear.

"What do we do now?" Heather replied calmly. No one answered her. None of them didn't want to talk for a while, now that they were lost. Hope was gone; nothing and no one seemed to care. They had no clue what was going to happen next. They were just hoping for something good to happen.

"It would be easier if we were following directions from a map," Tracy voiced out. David, Billy, Heather, and Josh both smiled at her. Tracy was the only one who ever lit things up in the group for them.

"It would be nice if you shut up."

"It would be nice if you shut up. Geez Sarah, what's wrong with you? You've been acting very different lately." They all had enough of Sarah's attitude.

"Lately? More like for a while. She's been acting like this for the past couple of months. I'm surprised that you noticed now," Josh pointed out.

"I'm not acting any different than any of you. I'm the one who always tries to light everything up with jokes and sarcasm. Now I'm being called crazy from you guys?"

"We're not saying that you're crazy. We just think that...."

"You know what I don't care what the fuck you think. If anybody is going to be acting crazy here is Tracy. None of us ever see her do anything anyway." Sarah turned in her seat. Sarah had made the biggest mistake of her life. If only she could take back what she had just said in front of Tracy's face, she could, but this time was different. Tracy just stared at her. They were all silent waiting for Tracy's reactions.

Tracy's eyes were empty, tears filled around the corner of her eyes. She couldn't stand Sarah as much as she couldn't stand Billy. She left without saying a word to anybody. David hardened his stare towards Sarah. Heather got angrier by the minute because of what Sarah said to Tracy. She couldn't believe that she said that to her. Heather knew that Tracy was the only one who ever lit anything up for the group not Sarah.

"Well I hope you're happy. You will regret this day I fuckin' swear it you will," David hardened his tone.

"Actually I am. And at least I'm not the one who made a mistake by dating a girl who is way out of my league," Sarah smiled, putting a little emphasis on the words.

"I swear to god I'm going to do something to you that you will make me regret for the rest of my life." His tone changed and Sarah's smile withered away. He jumped out of the car and followed Tracy. They watched their every movement. He put his arm around her and wiped away all her tears.

"Are you going to be okay now?" David asked with a smile and a little worry.

"I think so," Tracy wiped tears that formed under her eyes. She smiled back at him. He brought his hand to her face and wiped away the rest of the tears. His hand lingered on her face and he traced his fingers slowly down her face. He brought his lips to hers wanting everything to be okay.

"Come on, let's go back." He took her hand and led her back. When she didn't move he turned to her.

"What's wrong?" His smile withered away when she didn't want to go back.

"I don't want to go back."

"Why not?" Tracy gave him a look that said she didn't want anything else to happen.

"Come on. I got a better idea." David smiled once again and they went their own way. He wrapped his arms tight around her not wanting anything else happening to her. They didn't care what any of them thought, just as long as they were gone from Sarah and the look on her face.

Heather had nothing to say. If only she stood up for her, but she knew that Sarah would ignore her if she did. Josh made his own decision and jumped out of the car. Billy, Sarah, and Heather were the only ones left. They had no clue what was going to happen next, they could just only pray for something good to happen.

"So now what are we gonna do?" Sarah heaved. Billy turned to face her.

"I don't want to hear you talking right now. You ruined enough by whining and complaining. I'm sick and tired of your complaining. Try and do something productive with yourself other than thinking about yourself. You ruined everything from here," Billy had to get it out on the open. He couldn't take it anymore.

He couldn't stand her anymore. Sarah was getting on Billy's nerves. He could feel his temples beating harder by the second and his heart beating faster than the speed of light. He turned back to face the front and tried to forget what just happened in the last hour.

"Where do you think Josh, Tracy, David and Sean are?" Heather asked. Billy was thinking about the same thing.

"I have no clue." There was dead silence in the car. Without Tracy, Heather had no one to talk to. Billy put his hands on the ignition and started the car and waited for the car to take them back on the right road.

—∘∘∘◦❂◦∘∘∘—

Sean walked for a while and took a breath. His breathing was becoming labored and it was hard for him to breath. He stopped short in his tracks and took out his inhaler and breathed slowly and gradually. Just as his breathing returned, he heard footsteps behind him. They walked at the same pace as he did. When he stopped, they stopped. His feet pounded hard on the gravel road as he ran. The footsteps also ran at the same pace.

The running made him stop. He took out his inhaler again and breathed slowly. He caught his breath when he thought he heard the footsteps. He stayed quiet making sure that they were gone. There was nothing. He breathed in a sigh of relief and got himself to stand up after he fell. He continued walking again. When he stopped, he knew for sure that there was someone behind him. When he turned around, everything turned black.

"Are you okay buddy?" Josh lightly slapped his face. Sean woke up dizzy and lightheaded from what happened. He groaned and sat up quickly which only made the dizziness worse and he felt like someone was pushing him back into the darkness.

"What happened?" He looked around him. Not sure if he was in the same spot he was from before. It was dark and it was hard to make out where any of them were.

"I don't know. All I know is that someone was following me and I blacked out." They all stared at each other and wondered who would be following them. David and Tracy sat next to Sean. It all got quiet.

"What about Billy, Sarah, and Heather? Where do you suppose they are?" Tracy wondered she didn't even care about Sarah and Billy, but she was worried about Heather, not as if she was trying to feign interest at all in Sarah and Billy.

"I don't know. But I'm sure Sarah's at it again," Josh replied. They didn't even want to think about it. They were sick and tired of talking about them.

"At least I managed to save eight bottles though," Josh held up the bottles quickly changing the subject and the silence.

"So we got two bottles each," Sean laughed finishing off Josh's sentence.

"All right, all right. Enough bottle talk. Now would be a good time to get out of here rather than sitting here and talking with no purpose," David came in.

"Okay then, where shall we start from? I'm pretty sure you can lead us the way out of here, since you were the one who brought up the idea of leaving."

"I didn't come up with the idea of leaving. I just thought that it would be better to start walking our way the fuck out of here."

"All right then, lead the way." They all laughed at what Sean had said. In less than five minutes, they started walking and tried to find where freedom was.

CHAPTER 10

They walked on for quite a while, not knowing where they were or where they were going. They got restless with each passing time. They stopped for a while to rest since they were all tired.

"Does anybody have a match?" Sean wondered aloud.

"I thought you had since you smoke," Josh stretched the last syllables and laughed.

"Nah quit two years ago." Sean felt proud of himself.

"Yeah right. I'm sure something or someone stopped you." He pulled out a cigarette and smoked himself and stared at Sean and waited for him to say something.

"Nothing or no one made me stop. I just had the need to stop because; well because my mom smoked her entire life and I thought it's better to be myself than to be like my mother eh?" Sean replied and stared at Josh. Sean was trying not to stutter and stumble on any of the words.

"Yeah, I feel for you man. Too bad I don't feel that way," Josh patted his chest and started laughing after a while.

"I don't know why I even bother to tell anybody anything especially you, you're such a jerk." Josh just continued on laughing.

"Nah I really feel sorry for you buddy. You just gotta learn to let a part of you go when something like that happens in your life." Josh patted his back.

"Yeah I guess you're right. I just don't know what I'm going to do that's all."

"Yeah well sometimes... I don't care. Good luck with everything." Josh patted his back and started laughing. He moved away from Sean when he saw him give him a glare.

"How are we going to make a fire? There's not even any wood."

"Well then I guess we'll have to break you in half and burn you like hell," Sean laughed at his own joke. Josh looked at him and made a face. They both sat across from each other making faces at each other while they waited and wondered where David and Tracy were.

Sean, who was facing his way towards Josh, saw David and Tracy walking over carrying wood. They both smiled at Sean and he smiled back. He turned his gaze from them back to Josh who was taking out a second cigarette from behind his ear.

"What?" Josh asked dumbly.

"Nothing," Sean hid his smile from him. He turned back to David and Tracy who were right behind Josh. In seconds, they dropped the wood.

"What the...." Josh jumped up startled. They all laughed.

"Jerks," Josh cried out and walked away from them and their laughter.

"You had it coming." Their laughter echoed.

"Where did you find all this wood?" Sean was surprised at how much there was.

"If you just thought ahead and followed us.... you would've found something," Tracy smiled throwing down the last pile of wood that she carried in her arm. Behind her, David walked up and produced the last pile of wood.

Josh, who was in another world, came back to reality and turned around to face his friends. When he saw the amount of wood that was found and piled up in a bundle, his eyes almost popped out.

"What is this? We don't need all this wood. It's not like we're gonna live here," he dangled the cigarette in between his fingers and threw some of his ashes between some of the wood that was ready to be lit. They all stared at him in thought.

"And who said we're taking your advice?" David stared at him blankly.

"I did. Now let's pack up whatever we have, not that we have anything and leave." Josh started walking.

"Forget him, he's a loser anyway," Sean caught their stares as they watched him leave.

The twigs snapped in the fire, which made its sparks, threatening them with its anger. From time to time, they would listen to any noise in the distance. They thought that there was a breeze, but there was nothing. Somewhere deep in the deep far distance, an owl can be heard and scampering footsteps of some animal.

The sky revealed an overcast glow and blended with the fire as if the sky was burning with rage and fury. The stars lit up the sky, which was a good enough compass except the moon that hid itself away from the sight of it all. Josh finally made his way back towards them. He tried to sit comfortably on the gravel.

"'Bout time you came. Where were you?" David asked.

"That is none of your business." He sat down and pulled out another cigarette.

"Don't you think that you should stop smoking? I think you've had enough," Sean replied.

"I'll know when I've had enough. Now what's going on?" He puffed on his cigarette and threw some of the ashes in the fire. They just stared at him not knowing what to do. They tried to make him stop smoking but there is nothing and no one who can stop him. Tracy was fast asleep. Her head was rested on David's lap.

"I was thinking, what if Billy planned the trip the whole time? I mean we could've easily got tickets to go to Darwin on a plane, Billy wanted to drive," Sean thought. Both David and Josh thought for a moment.

"You know what, you're right. And for the first time in your life," Josh laughed along with David. Sean mocked their laughter.

"Oh you guys are so funny. No but seriously, think about it. We actually could have bought tickets to go to Darwin on a plane or a bus or whatever, but Billy wanted to drive." Now they were all silent. They didn't know what to think or say.

"So you're saying that Billy could be in on all this?" Josh raised his eyebrows.

"Why not? He made us come with him, and he didn't even know where he was going. I mean come on think about it he didn't even ask any of us for directions. Billy doesn't even know where anything is," Sean was starting to become suspicious.

David and Josh raised their eyebrows at him. But when he said that last sentence, they felt something inside. Tracy moved a bit, which made them hold their breaths for a while. They didn't want to tell her anything yet and they didn't want her to know anything until they had something.

"So you're saying that Billy is on all this?" David wondered. Sean and Josh both looked at him.

"Geeze man, you even said that I was smart. I thought you were smart," Sean laughed. David made a face at him.

"That's not where I'm going, and I am smart. I'm saying that after all this, we're going to blame Billy for something stupid that he didn't do? I mean come on; Billy wouldn't do anything stupid like that, would he?" David's voice rose in suspicion.

"Think about it man," Josh replied.

"I don't think he would do anything like that."

"You guys don't know him like I do. He'd do anything crazy just to piss us off."

"What did we ever do to him that would make him do this to us? Why would he want to piss us off for no reason? We never did anything to him."

"That's my point."

"What's your point? You have nothing. There's no reason why he would possibly do anything to us that would make us get on his nerves."

"I hate to interrupt but uh, I agree with Josh on this," Sean interfered. Sean and Josh both stared at David. If he wasn't going to think the same thing as them, they might as well leave him hanging. David thought about it. He knew that they were right about Billy and the way he always forgot where he was going.

"Yeah, I guess you guys are right. I'm just.... I don't know. It's just hard to think that he would do anything like this," David sighed.

"Yeah well buddy, that's life." They all sighed. Tracy lifted her head off David's lap and smiled at him. Josh got another cigarette from behind his other ear and Sean poked a stick in the fire. Tracy looked at them with a look on her face that said that they were up to something.

"Oh look who's finally up," Josh smiled. They all exchanged looks and they all laughed.

"What's so funny?" Tracy wondered.

"Nothing." Sean laughed harder so did Josh. Tracy folded her arms against her chest and her legs and sat beside David.

"What were you guys talking about?"

"Nothing," Sean replied quickly.

"Oh come on, I heard you guys talking."

"What do you think we were talking about? I mean what makes you think that we were talking?"

"Nothing really. I just thought I heard you say my name that's all." Josh walked away and breathed in a sigh of relief. There was silence between them. David rested beside the fire with Tracy while Sean and Josh kept a distance away from them trying to figure out what's going on.

"I don't know man. All I know is that we could try and deal with this on our own," Sean sighed. They both walked back towards the fire that glowed freely and dimly. Josh pulled out another pack of cigarettes and pulled out two. He put one behind his ear and the other he smoked.

"Don't you think that it's time that you stopped smoking?" Sean replied.

"Don't you think that it's time that you shut up?" Josh contradicted him. There was nothing that any of them can say or do to make him stop.

"When do you think we'll leave this damn place?" Josh thought a loud.

"When you stop talking through your nose," Sean laughed along with David and Tracy.

"Mock me if you will, but you guys will be paying for every sarcastic joke that you make at me." Sean, David, and Tracy all looked at each other and laughed. They were quiet for a while. Finally after what seemed like a long day, they slept on the hard ground. Tracy moved closer to David as he hugged her close, and Sean and Josh stayed up for a while to try and think about the things that are going on so far.

"So you actually think that Billy is going to hurt us?" Sean whispered to Josh.

"Well I don't know exactly though. But think about it, Billy would do anything to try and get attention,"

Josh whispered back. They stopped talking when Tracy moved a bit.

Sean and Josh moved away from them so they could think about it some more. Sean didn't know what exactly to think. Thoughts were racing through his mind one by one. They were sure that something was going to happen, but they didn't know when or where.

"What do you really think?" Josh stared at him intently.

"I don't really know what to think. But right now it's to keep this from Tracy before she finds out about what we were talking about today."

"Yeah well, I'm just trying to forget that he's even my brother."

"What do you mean?"

"Since that night we went to the bar, he's been acting crazy lately. He's been throwing tempers and he's got a bad attitude."

"I thought he's perfect. Good enough for anything gets good grades and doesn't fool around...." Josh interrupted him.

"Just because Billy is perfect doesn't really mean he is perfect. He shows off when he can and he tried to beat me in everything. Did I tell you what happened a couple of weeks ago?" Sean shook his head.

"Our parents went out a couple of weeks ago and took my brother and sister to some party or whatever the hell. Anyways after they left, Billy went into the garage and found the packs of cigarettes and the full bottles and took them to his room and drank them all, in one night. After that, he started to go crazy. He pulled everything down threw a really bad temper and was throwing things around."

"Anyways I told him to stop, but he wouldn't. After that, things started to get worse but our parents didn't find out about it yet. I'm hoping that they will stumble in reality and finally realize the things that he's been doing and hiding from them," Josh went quiet after a while. It was dead silence, the night had no breeze, and the sky was starting to change.

"Yeah well, I wish none of this had happened in the first place."

"It's all up to us now," Josh nodded his head in agreement. Just then a loud scream erupted. There were muffled voices from a distant. Sean and Josh ran towards Tracy and David. They weren't there.

"Where did they go?" Sean thought aloud and realized that it was a stupid question to ask.

Another scream broke through the night. They ran toward the noise. They were shocked to see David sprawled on the ground and Tracy being dragged. David tried holding his grip on Tracy's but the other guy was strong enough and pulled her away. But the more she tried, the harder the other guy kept pulling his grip on her. Tracy dragged her fingernails along the ground hoping for some help from Sean and Josh. Josh made his way toward the guy while Sean went after David.

"Hey man, are you okay?"

"Yeah I'm fine. What about Tracy, where's Tracy?" David tried getting up. He saw Josh fighting with the guy while Tracy was trying to leave but couldn't. David tried running toward them. Sean saw him limp his way toward them. The guy finally broke free and slung Tracy over his shoulder and ran with a limp.

"Stay here," Sean told David.

Both Sean and Josh ran after him and caught up to him. Just as they reached him, they saw him rip Tracy's clothes off. They both stared at each other. Sean ran up to them and he jumped on the guy punching him each time. The guy kept slapping him trying to break free from Sean's grip. He had a strong grip on him. Nothing seemed to break his concentration when he was fighting with someone or fighting for something. When he fought with him, the thought of his mom appeared which made him punch the guy harder each time.

Josh held on to Tracy's hand and they both ran from him. Josh came back to find the guy struggling under Sean's grip. One punch was all Sean gave to give the guy a bleeding nose. He finally let go when he heard the guy cry out. The guy could barely run. He limped with two bad legs while he clutched his shoulder that was shooting with pain.

"Yeah you better run you fuckin' bastard," Sean cried. They watched him leave. They went back to make sure that Tracy was okay. They found her wrapped in David's arm.

"You okay?" He asked her with a shaky voice.

"Yeah, I'm fine. I'm fine," she wiped away her tears and lifted her head up and smiled at him. They both smiled at each other. She wiped away her tears and dug herself deeper into his hug. Everything was dead silent no one said a word to each other until Tracy was fast asleep. In the brightness of the fire, David and Josh noticed deep marks on Sean's face.

"What happened?" Sean fingered the scratches on his face.

"Nothing much happened just as long as he got what he deserved, that fuckin' bastard. If he comes back again, I swear to god I'm going to kill him," Sean clenched his jaw and it was hard for him to talk because of the marks on his face made themselves deeper.

"What a night huh?" Josh replied sullenly. They all agreed with him. They all looked at each other with looks on their faces that were saying that they couldn't stand it much longer.

"What are we going to do now?" Sean wondered aloud. They all shook their heads wondering the same thing.

CHAPTER 11

Sarah and Heather were quiet. Not a word was said between the three of them. They were just anxious to get out and leave. Just then, Billy stopped.

"Why did you stop?" Sarah cried.

"I'm not leaving without David, Sean, Josh, and Tracy."

"Who cares? They're gone they're not going to come back."

"NO," he banged his hand on the dashboard and everything got quiet. He quickly got out of the car and wanted to get away from everything. He didn't know what to do. Sarah looked at Heather through the rearview mirror. She looked at her with a look on her face saying that enough happened already in one night. Instead, Sarah moved toward the drivers' seat.

"Wait. What about Billy?"

"I could care less about him right now." Sarah tried starting the car as they drove off trying to find a way out. Heather shook her head in disbelief at her. She couldn't believe that any of this was happening. If only she left with them, she wouldn't be in this situation with Sarah. They drove around trying to find a way out. It was useless. There was no way out. Each direction they went through only made it worse. They didn't know where they were and they didn't know where they were getting to. Sarah finally shut the engine off thinking that there was nowhere to go and no one to ask. They were well into being afraid.

"What are we going to do now?" Heather seemed to echo Josh as if they knew what each other were thinking. She missed Josh. She missed his laugh and his smile that made her happy. She missed the way he used to love her.

They both stared at the empty night. The stars seemed innocent; they glittered on ignoring the cries and their voices. The moon didn't bother to show that night. It was empty and dull and the sky was nothing without the moon. Sarah and Heather shivered from the cold even though there was no wind that they could feel.

"There's nothing we can do....yet," Sarah's voice sounded cold. Anything she said never had the nerve to have sarcasm or any jokes in it. There was bitter silence in the night that seemed to suit their attitude for everything that seem to happen all at once or things that already happened. Footsteps in the night caught their attention.

"Who's there?" Sarah's voice shivered. The footsteps stopped at the sound of her voice even though they were far away. They seemed to know when to stop and went to go. Sarah and Heather looked at each other both shaking in anticipation for something to happen.

"Maybe it's Billy."

"I doubt it's even Billy. He left like an hour ago. As if he would come back." They turned around to find no one there. The footsteps continued again. The footsteps got louder and closer toward them.

"Come on Heather get out of the car."

"What?"

"I said get out. We'll both get out, come on." They both got out stumbling on their own. They both stretched out. Sarah tried to smooth out her clothes.

"We don't have time for that Sarah, what if we get caught?" Heather realized what she said was a mistake. Sarah looked up and stared at her.

"So what if we get caught?"

"What if it's only Billy?"

"Billy, are you serious? He left like ten hours ago. You seriously think that he's going to come back?" Heather shook her said.

"I wasn't saying that. I just thought....." Heather lost her voice and couldn't even finish her sentence. Heather choked on her breath and couldn't breathe. Sarah turned around to tie her shoes that she didn't realize that Heather stopped talking.

"What were you thinking huh? That we might get killed or something. I mean, come on Heather don't take it all so serious." Sarah turned around and gasped in horror. Heather was strangled around the neck and she couldn't breathe. Her face was turning purple and the blood was all rushing to her head and she could see that her veins were popping out.Sarah was about to scream, but he moved toward her and silenced her.

"You scream and I'll fuckin' kill both of you," he whispered in her ear. Heather struggled in his grasp. The more she struggled with him, the tighter his grip became around her.

"Get in the car," he shoved Sarah and Heather in the car. Sarah sat in the front in the drivers' seat while he sat in the back with Heather.

"Drive," he replied. He cocked a gun to her head and she heard it click. Sarah had no idea what kind of trouble they were going through. Sarah put them in the situation and she had to get them out. She was shaking trying to decide whether or not they should go through it. Sarah gently moved her head to the right and caught Heather's gaze in the mirror. Tears were streaming down her face. Her eyes were shut tight praying that none of it was real, when she opened her eyes, nothing changed.

"DRIVE NOW." He held the gun closer to her and was about to shoot. She turned her head around and put her hands on the ignition and started the car. Before she started the car, she looked through the rearview mirror and caught a glimpse of Heather's eyes. They seemed to share similar expressions and thoughts towards each other. He pushed the gun harder against her skull and her head leaned against the window. If she didn't do what he wanted, he was going to kill them both. She started the car and drove to where ever he wanted to go.

There was silence in the night between the four campers. Nothing seemed right anymore for them because of the trip. They all sighed aloud waiting for some kind of sign for anything.

"I would give anything to be home right now," David sighed. They all nodded in agreement.

"I would give anything to be in England," Josh sighed in deep thought. They all stared at him in amazement at him.

"What?" he threw and exasperated look.

"After being lost in the middle of nowhere and getting into some crap, you still want to go to England?" Sean looked at him.

"Well yeah. I mean, not by car if that's what you're thinking. That was Billy's idea to come by car instead of an airplane to Darwin. You're such a loser."

"You're the loser," Sean picked at some remains of the fire that was still burning and threw it at him. Josh dodged out of the way.

"I don't know about that. I don't really see any loser here but you. And don't try to hide it because I know everything about you."

"You know nothing about me."

"Oh yeah. Let me explain to you the life of Sean and how he lives," Josh turned to David and Tracy and put on a play for them. They laughed at him. Sean's face turned red.

"We all know that Sean is rich. He lives a happy life with his mother, but there is one thing that we don't know exactly about his mother...."

"OKAY, okay. Nobody needs to know right now," Sean interrupted him.

"I want to know. Come on," Tracy pleaded.

"Yeah come on Sean you're wrecking it for us." David pitched in and they all laughed.

"You know what fine. Make your little play, because I don't care anymore." Sean turned and walked off.

"Oh come on man, were just joking." But to him it was no joke.

As he walked away from them, he realized that all his life was his mother. A part of his life was ripped away from him because of his mother. He didn't want to believe the things that she said and did to him. He also didn't want to believe the truth about anything. He loved his mother yet at the same time he didn't. He shut his eyes tight and tried ignoring it, but the image of his mother didn't disappear.

"Look man, I didn't mean any of that. You know I was joking," Sean didn't notice that Josh was behind him.

"Yeah, don't worry about it man. We're with you all the way," David smiled at him. Josh busted out laughing.

"I'm sorry man. I just...." He couldn't stop laughing. David punched him in the arm and Josh punched him back. They struggled with each other as they made their way back. He watched them walk the rest of the way. He sighed heavily and walked back towards his friends. He sat with his head in his hands.

"Are you okay Sean?" Tracy smiled at him. He lifted his head up and smiled back at her.

"Yeah, I'm fine."

"Are you sure, you don't look okay,"

"Don't worry about me. I'll be fine." He smiled at her to reassure her that he was okay and she smiled back. That night was like any other night that they had at the same spot.

"What a night huh? Spitting nothing but jokes and fights over each other."

"Yeah well, I just want to leave from this damn place that I call hell," Josh cried.

They all agreed that it was no place for them and it was no place to have fun, but they tried to make it fun. They just couldn't wait to leave the place and go home. Nothing was easy for them, they didn't know how they got lost and they also did not know how they were going to find a way out.

CHAPTER 12

In the dark, nothing moved. Not a sound was heard except the heavy breathing. It was pitch dark with no lights lit up anywhere, not even the bright light of the moon. Sarah couldn't breathe. Her body felt numb all over. She didn't know what happened; she tried to think back to what exactly happened but no memory came to her. She didn't know exactly where they were, she just wanted to get out. She tried to move, but couldn't, something seemed to be holding her back.

A dimly lit light, bounced off the walls from somewhere behind her. She turned around to see if there was someone was there but there was nobody. She looked around and saw the light bounce off the walls and the covered windows, the light also bounced off the chains. When she saw them, she gasped in horror. She struggled with the chains. She tried calling out but no noise came from her. She turned to see if Heather was there, but she wasn't. She couldn't breathe.

She banged her head against the heavy metal pole behind her, which only made things worse for her. She cried in agony from the pain that she received. Her head was starting to hurt badly. She lifted her arm to try and see if there was any blood, but she couldn't. She didn't know what to do, the only thing that was left for her to do was to try and make noise for somebody to hear her and help her. Finally, with little effort and little noise, someone came.

"Do you not know how to shut the fuck up?" he watched her slump from movement.

"Oh boy, do I ever have a surprise for you like your friend who enjoyed it peacefully and gratefully. Oh I can't wait I just don't know about you." He moved away from her and left. Her eyes went wide in disbelief and thought to herself. Thoughts were going throughout her mind about Heather. She didn't know what she was going to do to herself. She could only wish that they were back in the car leaving from the place that they were in.

The same guy came in and stood before her. He stared at her carefully and traced her figure with his fingers. She shivered and tried backing away only she couldn't. He laughed quietly. He moved closer to her and whispered in her ear.

"I hope you like the surprise that I have for you. Your friend enjoyed it more than I did," he leered into her face and forcefully took the tape off her mouth. Sarah screamed when he did that. He just stared at her and laughed.

"What did you do to my friend?" words barely came out of her mouth as she coughed and tried to catch her breath.

"Nothing in particular. Just something that I thought might cheer her up," he smiled again with his teeth showing. He moved his fingers across her face.

"Don't touch me," Sarah tried jerking away from him. The chains rattled from her movement.

"You know as I well as I do that I can't obey to that," he chuckled moving his fingers down her neck. Sarah breathed heavily. She wanted to run but she knew that she couldn't.

"Now you know very well that I can't let you leave unless you do what I tell you to do," he replied as if he knew what she was thinking. Sarah tried calming down a bit.

"What did you to my friend," Sarah was on the verge of tears.

"Nothing you really need to know about. I can give you the details but I can't tell you where she is," He smiled again only this time it wasn't like any other smile.

"You're sick," Sarah cried out.

"No. She was sick."

"How would you know? You had her tied up and taped up like me."

"You know what; you're starting to get on my damn nerves." He moved closer to her and put the tape back on her mouth.

"Sweet dreams," he whispered in her ear and shoved his tongue in her ear. Sarah cried in alarm. She wanted to leave; she wanted somebody to find her. She moaned one last time, which was only a moan of pain and agony.

Billy walked on forever trying to find his way out. He found himself walking towards a gas station. He shut his eyes and opened them thinking that it was just a mirage, or a dream of some sort but it wasn't. Billy ran the rest of the way to the gas station. He reached the door and went inside. He walked around the store looking for somebody.

"Hello." Nobody answered.

"Hello?" Still there was no answer. He left and went outside and walked to the back there was no one there. It seemed strange that no one was there. He went back in and tried looking for someone. He went to the back of the store and tried looking for someone.

"Hello." There was still no answer to his reply. He moved farther in. He turned around and made sure that no one was there and moved on. The light dimmed on until there was no light. Every step he took brought him further to where he wanted to go. The furnace buzzed on and he jumped from the noise. He continued on with his way. He finally reached the end, which only led to outside of the gas station. He closed the door and went back inside. As he reached the front of the place, someone jumped up in front of him. Billy gasped.

"What were you doing back there boy, huh?"

"I....I was just...." his voice trailed off and he walked away from him. Billy left with a more than a handful of food and more than two bottles and ran as the guy chased him.

"If you ever come back here I will kill you," he screamed at Billy. Billy finally was out of earshot away from him. He turned around only to find him gone from the doorway.

He walked the rest of the way trying to breathe. He finally found a spot to sit and relax. He popped open one bottle and opened a package of candy. He sat there wondering about his friends. He remembered he saw David, Sean and Tracy with a place of their own. Even though there was no wind, he was cold. He shivered in his shoes debating on whether if he should stay or not. He knew better than to stay in a spot where someone might find him and kill him, so he went his way going through a shortcut and made a couple of turns and kept on going throughout the night until he found the road.

CHAPTER **13**

Finally, they had enough. It was time for them to leave the place and forget the things that ever happened. Tracy, David, and Sean took whatever they needed and left. They walked on trying to find someone or a place where they could actually stay the night without having to sleep on the hard ground with the small and big rough jagged rocks.

"I can't wait to get home," Sean threw an exasperated sigh.

"Will you stop talking about it? You're making me tired." David seemed to have enough of him.

"You're not the only one that's tired," Josh put in. Tracy said nothing as she walked alongside David holding his hand. There was a long moment of silence between them. It was quiet under the hot sun. Sean held his side leaning on his right side and holding himself down to relax.

"Hurry up man. There's a lot more snails that are moving faster than you," Josh called out and laughed. Their laughter trailed along the air giving some life. Sean stopped completely. He felt triggering hard against his chest and couldn't breathe. He tried to relax and breathe deeply and normally, but he couldn't. He reached for his inhaler in his pockets, it wasn't there. The rest of his friends stopped and turned around to see what he was doing.

"What are you doing man? Hurry up." Josh called out.

"N....Nothing. I'm j....just trying to look...." He called back but his voice trailed along and he felt like he was losing his voice.

"I....I'll be right back." He tried raising voice a bit louder, but he couldn't, his voice was just a small whisper. Sean turned around and dropped his eyes on the ground looking for his inhaler. He practically looked everywhere. He traced back their trail of where they were the last time. He still couldn't find it. His breathing became labored and he felt like he was going to faint. From a distance, Josh, David and Tracy could tell that he wasn't feeling good and knew that he wasn't up for anything.

"Josh stay here with Tracy, I'll be right back." David jogged his way towards Sean and caught up to him to see what was going on. They stopped and turned around to see what was going on.

"Hey Sean, what's going on man?" David saw him waver back and forth. He closed his eyes and tried to relax. Sean moved his gaze towards something and moved forward towards it.

"Sean. Come on don't do this to us." David caught a glimpse of what Sean was looking at. Sean's footsteps became smaller each time and his knees were giving in. David moved toward the object and saw what he was looking at. He picked up his inhaler and gave it to him.

"Come on man." He looked at him and gave him his inhaler. His face was pale pale and he couldn't dare to look at his face. Sean put it close to his mouth. Just as he was about to breathe, he collapsed with no air in him. David pushed him on his side which made the air come straight out of him. He quickly gave him his inhaler and breathed deeply until his breathing became rhythmic. Sean got up ever so slowly and tried to relax and get his breathing right.

"Are you okay man?" Sean felt dizzy a bit but managed to get up and walk.

"I'll be fine."

"You sure?" Sean nodded. They walked back towards their friends with no talk between them. When David reached Tracy, he took her hand and held on to it tighter than before.

"Are you okay David?" She saw him worry in thought. He didn't say anything because he was too deep in thought. He shook his head and smiled at Tracy.

"I'm fine." He hugged her close.

They walked on forever in silence under the heat of the sun. Finally under all the strain and the heat, they collapsed. They had enough of walking and they wanted to just leave.

"I'm sick and tired of this I wanna go home," Josh complained.

"We gotta try to stick out from here come on man, get up and lets go before something happens to someone again," Sean tried to grin and beret. David stopped in midway realizing that Sean and Josh were no longer behind them.

"Hurry up guys." He stopped and waited for them. He watched them get into a heated discussion with each other and went to go cool it off.

"What the hell is wrong with you?" Sean replied to Josh.

"Nothing's wrong with me. It's just you that gets on my damn nerves every time we go somewhere."

"Well let's try and go somewhere this time without you bothering me"

"Geeze guys what's wrong with you?" David came up to them.

"Ask him," Josh walked away.

"What do you mean "ask him." You're the one that started it all."

"Okay, that's enough," David tried breaking in through.

"Not Sean."

"You know what I had enough of you. From here on in I'm gonna pretend that you're not my friend and I'm gonna pretend that the things you said are worth nothing to me," Sean yelled at him.

David wanted to break the fight yet at the same time he didn't want to get involved in something that didn't include him. When Sean got up, Josh pulled him down and fought him again. They both got up and fought like crazy. They each had a bleeding nose and one of their noses looked like it was broken. One of their arms also looked like it was broken but no one could really tell. Finally David had to break their fight, he had enough of them.

"Just stop it. Nothing is going to turn anything around. Just relax. We all had a rough time. We could use a break we've walked enough." David turned and walked away. They both stared at David who slumped down on the hard ground.

"This is all your fault." Josh turned away and walked back from where they first started. Sean walked towards David. There was silence between them both.

"I'm sorry we got in a fight."

"Yeah well this is the first fight I've heard in my life between you two."

"I was uh, how do say it, I was trying to tell him to relax and to calm down for a while. But unlike him he doesn't listen to anybody. I don't know what I'm going to do." David just sat there listening and thinking deep in thought. They both stopped talking. Everything was still. Without Josh, they had nothing to do, nothing to say.

"Where's Tracy?" Sean thought aloud. David's eyes bulged out and almost forgot about her. David walked towards the spot she was before, she wasn't there.

"Tracy?" He couldn't find her. Sean watched Josh walk back from his walk. He could see that his face was red and his eyes were bloodshot. He ignored him and helped David look for Tracy. Josh jogged back the rest of the way to see what was going on.

"What's wrong?"

"Just shut up," Sean casted an angry glare at him.

"Let's not start this again." David was growing impatient with them.

"You know what I actually felt sorry for you, but now, you can just fuck off."

"Yeah well I don't need anybody to feel sorry for me. I don't need you feeling sorry for me."

"Oh for crying out loud. Just shut up for once. We're not going to get anywhere with the two of you fighting. Let's just try and find Tracy and get the hell out of here." When David turned around Tracy stood there smiling.

"Where were you?" David smiled back.

"Somewhere. Come on there's something have to show you." Tracy took a hold of his hand and led the way. Sean followed them with an angry look on his face with Josh behind with his head down. They walked on for a while with no talk between them. Finally they came up on a place.

"I was walking for a while and this place came up and I thought if there's someone in the house we could get directions and they could help us," Tracy replied breaking the silence that seemed to go on forever.

"We could use the help."

"Are you kidding? Maybe they won't help us who knows maybe their serial killers or something," Josh thought a loud.

"Is that the only thing that you can think of right now, killing? What's wrong with you?"

"What's wrong with you?"

"The fact that the only thing you can think of is killing and nothing decent for once in your life."

"Actually I can think unlike you who can't even sit for at least five seconds."

"Oh please you're one to talk." Sean muttered something under his breath. Tracy stopped in mid stride and came up to them.

"What's wrong?"

"Ask him," Sean pointed toward Josh. Josh had the nerve to hit him so bad.

"I'm gonna kill you one day. Just watch." Sean just ignored him.

"Look. Just listen to me for once if you're not gonna listen to each other. We left Sarah, Heather, and Billy for a reason. I had a reason why I left, do any of you? I don't really need you to answer that but consider it. We put our life in danger and right now we have to put a fight on hold before we are able to go home and relax. Just calm down for now. We're going to go and see if anybody is in that house and we're gonna ask them for help. Just be thankful that we got this far," Tracy interrupted them and told them off. She had them thinking for a while and they all were quiet. She walked away and took David's hand and the two of them led the way.

Sean and Josh were both quiet. They didn't know what to say to each other. Even though they were both angry at each other, they felt sorry for one another. Josh seemed to know what Sean was thinking because they felt ignorant and stupid and selfish for yelling at each other for no reason. They fought for no reason and they yelled at each other only to get their anger out towards each other. No one said a word until they reached the house.

"So who wants to go first?" David looked at the rest of them with a grin on his face.

"Don't look at me," Sean cried.

"How about you Josh?"

"Why me?"

"Because you were the one who said that they might be killers." Sean had a big smile on his face. He knew he caught something. He didn't say a word. There was nothing that he could do so he gave in. They all watched Josh walk towards the door.

Josh walked carefully and slowly. He looked back at his friends and they just smiled at him and encouraged him. He turned around and headed slowly towards the door. As he ascended the big heavy stairs, he breathed heavily in anticipation. Finally he reached the front of the door. He lifted the solid heavy brass knocker and let it fall. The sound of it seemed to have echoed more than ten times in the dark empty house. He stood there for about a minute and waited.

"Well no one's home," he turned around and smiled at his friends, glad that no one was there. Behind him the door opened slowly and carefully. He turned around to see who it was.

"How may I help you?" A man no more than his late twenties early thirties looked a lot older than his age. To them, he looked as is he was in his seventies. He gave a gentle and warm smile that welcomed them and made them feel a bit safer from all the things that happened. He was not too tall and not too short. His features were empty and dull. Gray peaks formed around behind his ears. He looked like he was balding. His eyes looked cat-like with a short nose that barely stuck out.

His lips were cracked around the edges and his skin looked cracked for a guy like him at his age. He seemed like someone who was willing help four strangers standing in his doorway. Sean, David, and Tracy just stared at each other with a look on their faces wondering if they could depend on him helping them. They had a choice. One of those choices was taken out. They had enough of sleeping on the hard ground; they wanted to sleep on something warm and comforting. They all looked at each other once more until one of them spoke breaking the tension and the nervousness.

"Uh yeah. We were just looking for some help. We've been lost for a while and we were just hoping that we'd stumble by anyone or a house for some help and directions back to the main highway," David answered.

"Come in come in. I'd be glad to help. Come on in," he gestured them inside. They stood there in the doorway. Their mouths agape from the sight of the old man and how quickly he let them in.

"Come on in. I'm not going to let four young beautiful strangers stand in my doorway with no food in you. Come on." They just shrugged and walked in one by one. When they entered the big place, they all gasped in amazement. The place was big they were amazed to see that a person like him lived in a house like this one. The walls were covered with wallpaper rather than being painted. There was no furniture in one of the living rooms as they walked in.

They walked into the kitchen where it was bigger. There were no windows except for a door on the other side that led outside. There was a pantry that led to the back and kept going to who knows where. The kitchen was clean with nothing in it. They walked into another living room that only had one couch and four bay windows out looking the view.

"Come on sit please. Ask me anything if you'd like. You'd be pleased about the things I have seen, the people I've seen and many things and people that I see come and go from various places," he replied with a grin that showed his teeth. His teeth looked rotten and decayed from the inside of his mouth. His gums were swollen and red and his tongue was split in half. Tracy turned away when she saw his tongue slithering out from time to time whenever he talked. They were afraid to ask him anything. They were afraid that they might do something to tick him off and killing them.

"Uh.... no we're fine. We were just hoping if we can have some answers and leave as soon as we can," David stumbled on his words and stuttered.

"Please come and sit. I haven't seen people for a really long time. I'd like to have company for a couple of days. Maybe for a couple of weeks."

Again his teeth showed and his tongue slipped out and he sucked it back in. He made a slurping noise that made Tracy cover her ears and turn away from the sight of him. He moved toward Tracy and stared at her.

"So tell me, what are your names," he slithered his tongue back and forth. David, Josh and Sean tried to stick it out with him; they knew that Tracy was already shivering in her shoes. Sean did most of the talking for them. Sean introduced them to him. As he did, the stranger's eyes fell on Tracy's and couldn't get his eyes off of her. He licked his teeth and brushed his tongue against his cheeks.

"You are beautiful I can see that," his smile was nothing but a snarl.

"She's my girlfriend," David stepped in holding her close. He didn't take his eyes off of her. He stepped closer towards her. She could smell the stench of rotting food in his mouth.

"I'd love to get me a girlfriend like you. I would be giving her all that she needs and let her feel satisfied about it all," He whispered to her, his mouth on her ear. David held her hand and Tracy tightened her grip around him. He went up to her and tried to capture every part of her.

"You smell soo good." Josh knew there was something wrong. He quickly stopped him from doing anything else and intervened.

"So, uh, how long did you say you lived here?" He quickly turned around and stared at Josh.

"Pardon me?" He replied pretending that he wasn't listening.

"How long have you been living here for?" David released a sigh of relief, while Tracy was still holding her breath even though he was nowhere near her.

"My whole life actually. My parents thought that this was the house that they wanted and it turns out it is. They wanted to live in a house that overlooked a beautiful sight and they ne'er took their eyes away. They lived a dream that they wanted. They had seven kids; I'm the youngest of them."

"However, on a sad occasion, they died of a fatal car accident. My parents and my four older brothers died and they suffered a lot. My mom had cancer that time and none of the doctors could help her they only prescribed her pills that made the pain worse each time. My father, well, he was rehab for over a couple of years. They realized it was stupid for him going in every two years, so they just took him out. Ever since, he never did anything bad.

"Now it's just me and my three other brothers livin' here in a place that we call home. We were lucky that we weren't in that accident. We prey for them everyday and night. Oh well, life goes on and we have to live with it eh? Well now that's enough about me why don't you each tell me a little about yourselves?" He grinned.They were all silent for a minute they had to reflect on what he just said.

"We're actually a bit tired. We had a long walk from where we were and we just need to rest for a bit," Sean finally came in.

"Oh sure of course. Where are my manners? My brothers always reminded me of manners whenever we got company which was rarely anymore. This is the first time we got company in years. This way please." They all stared at him not sure about what to do. They were crying inside and wanted to leave. They didn't care about how bad the place was they just wanted to leave. They followed him anyways; they needed something to sleep on rather than the hard ground. They stopped midway in the hallway at the end of the wing. Before he allowed one of them in at a time, Sean spoke up.

"Can we have a room for two people not just one for each person?" Sean backed away trying to catch a glimpse of his look. His eyes twitched and his eyebrows lowered.

"Sure. Of course you can," he hid whatever expression he had. Both Sean and Josh took the room they stood beside for about fifteen minutes, David and Tracy took the room next to them. When he left, they all breathed in a sigh of relief. Both Sean and Josh made sure that he wasn't in the hallway and went in the room where David and Tracy were.

"So what do you think?" Josh broke the tension between them.

"I think we should leave now," David looked at him.

"We just got here how can we leave when he's literally watching over us?"

"You're the one who said that we shouldn't be here in the first place and now you're changing your mind?"

"He said he could help us."

"They all say that. That's how they get you lured in the house and they kill you in the end," Josh brought in.

"I think we should leave tomorrow. Tracy's scared enough and I don't want to see her scared anymore. We came here uninvited and that freak is saying that he's been expecting people. We've had enough from here and I think we should leave," David announced. They whispered to each other so no one could hear them. They all agreed and stood there in silence wondering what was going to happen next.

"I just hope that we can find our way back home soon." They were all thinking the same thing. The one thing that was important to them right now was trying to get rid of the guy and leave the place before something happened to them. They didn't even have the chance to eat anything, but that seemed to be the least of their worries. Sean and Josh quietly left the room and went into theirs. They checked the hallway the first thing and quickly ran to the other room.

"I don't know if I can keep this up anymore," Sean complained sitting on a bed. "Well you're going to have to until we leave and go home." They both got under the covers in different beds. It was silent for a while.

"Hey Josh what do you think what's gonna happen next when we get home?" Sean brought up out of nowhere.

"Are you trying to get us in trouble or something?" He got up and stared at Sean. "No I just...." Sean lost his trial of thought.

"Why what are you trying to do," he said with a grin. "Nothing. I just wanna know that's all."

"Don't worry about it man. Just relax." "What you're not worried or anything?"

"I'm just tired about the things that have already happened. It's getting on my nerves. I'm just hoping nothing will spring out on us again. Just relax and try not to think about it. Just hope that tomorrow is a perfect day and that damn freak doesn't eat us alive." Josh finally went to sleep. Sean lay awake in bed trying to figure out where they were. At that moment for about five minutes, it felt like old times where it was him, Josh, Billy, and David used to talk quietly and laugh and Sean's mom never used to find out.

They were really best friends, yet there was something that was breaking their friendship apart. Only it was him, David, Tracy, and Josh who were the only ones left. It was only Sean and Josh who were the only ones who occupied the room with nothing to say. No laughter or cries erupted from them. Sean breathed in a heavy sigh and tried to relax. Not only did he not want to go home, he didn't want tomorrow to come.

CHAPTER 14

Billy thought it was the right road that might lead him out, but it wasn't. He only made it worse for himself as he drew in farther down the road. When he turned around he found himself lost in the midst. He went in different directions looking for a way out, but it was no use. He walked on for a while which made him think for more than just a minute.

He didn't know where he was going. He raged on in the darkness. He wanted someone or something to hear him but he knew that his screams meant nothing. He made up his mind and continued on walking. He fought with himself from time to time trying to figure out where the road was and which way led out. It took him a while to relax and try to think. He rested once again longer than before.

He sat there, thinking about Tracy. He felt sorry for her much more than he felt sorry for Sarah. He had a way to stop her talking to Tracy like that. For some reason he didn't. There was nothing stopping him to yell at Sarah to stop. He regretted every moment in the car sitting there quietly while the rest of the guys were protecting her.

The more he thought about it, the angrier he got. His mind raced angrily and he rubbed his head hard giving himself a headache. He was thinking of how it was a mistake to go driving to Darwin. We should've gone on the plane; we should've gone on the plane. He knew that Tracy and Heather's idea was better. He was driving himself crazy with all the thoughts that raged inside his head. He finally had enough and stood up and started walking.

He walked no more than ten feet and he heard noise. He turned around to see where the noise was coming from, but at night, the noise seemed to echo in different directions. He heard it again, this time it was in front of him. He heard the noise again, this time he heard it in the right direction. He turned around in circles not knowing where the noise was coming from. Finally he gave in he scrunched his hair in his hands thinking that he was only hallucinating and that there was nothing there.

But the noise continued on screeching and didn't stop. He tried to relax; he closed his eyes and opened them thinking that it was just a dream, but it wasn't. Dizzy from all the turmoil and the noise, he fell to the ground unconscious. The noise stopped and footsteps ran quickly and watched him sleep in a sea of nightmares.

CHAPTER 15

Sarah's voice was muffled from the tape that was around her mouth. She tried struggling, moving her arms and her legs around to get rid of the numbness. Sweat poured down her face and she was getting scared. About ten feet away, there was someone standing there behind her. She knew it was the same guy; she just wanted him to let her go. She didn't do anything wrong.

She stopped struggling and heard him approach her with caution. When she saw his face, it wasn't the same guy like she predicted. His face was covered in a mask and continued on walking. She wasn't even sure if it was a guy or not. There was another guy behind him and he led him the way to a room. It was the same guy. She stared at him intently. When he stopped in front of her, he removed the tape from her mouth and she screamed. He slapped her face.

"Shut up or I'll put this back on your mouth," he shouted hoarsely and loudly. She breathed heavily and tried to relax. She knew she couldn't relax. One way or another he had to let her go.

"Don't move," he demanded to the person in front of him. He moved toward Sarah and released the chains off of her. Sarah was confused yet at the same time she was happy.

"Don't even think about leaving," he whispered right in her face. She felt the hot breath of his on her face. He moved away from her and led the person to a room. She inspected him moving her head to a side. When the guy reached the room, he didn't close the door instead, he left it open. He placed the person on the bed and took off the mask.

Sarah got up wanting to see what was going on. Her legs felt numb from the discomfort because they were chained up. She didn't seem to care about the pain that vibrated through her legs and up to her arms. She winced from the pain each time she walked. At the door, she watched him remove the mask that hid the guy's face. She tried to get a closer look at who it was. When Sarah saw who it was, she gasped in horror.

"Billy?" she gasped. He lifted his head and cocked his head to the side and stared at her intently. She moved closer and saw the other guy with a saw in his hand.

"Say bye," he grinned at her. He moved the blade of the saw towards his head and chopped it off. "BILLY!!!!" She cried out. Blood spattered everywhere in the room. He cackled and raised his arms again and cut off every limb in his body. Now that she wasn't chained up, she was able to leave. Yet at the same time she didn't want to. She got scared from the look that Billy had on his face. She saw the guy get rid of the hair by shaving it all. She winced at the sight. She stood there for at least ten minutes watching him.

She gasped heavily and moved away from the gruesome sight. She scanned the area looking for a set of staircase. Her eyes stopped in the middle of the room and saw stairs leading up. She tried running toward them but she couldn't. Her legs that were tied up for so long were numb to the floor and she could barely move. She took one small step at a time hoping that by the time she gets to the stairs he'll still be in the room. She walked ever so slowly yet at the same time she tried to quicken her pace.

She stopped when she heard no noise coming from the room. She tried walking back toward the room where the guy was. She saw him lift his head up without the eyes, the nose and the mouth and saw him carrying his heart that was still beating and crushed it with one hand and blood spewed in his face. Sarah was disgusted. She turned away and vomited from the sight that she saw. When she turned to look back, he wasn't there. She quickly moved away from the room.

Her legs were still a bit numb. This time she moved quickly. She didn't care if her legs were hurting her and she didn't care about the pain throbbing in her legs and arms. Her breathing quickened and she couldn't catch up with her breathing. She looked around the room and saw that all the windows were barricaded with bars. There was one window that caught her attention. She quickly moved toward it. It didn't have anything covering it.

She looked around to make sure he wasn't there. The pain was getting worse in her arms and legs. She cried in alarm and fell back from the pain. She moved up toward the window and tried to open it. It was shut tight and it wouldn't open. Her arms squeezed tight against the window pane and her fingers were wrapped tight against the end of the window and she pushed it open. Little by little, the window opened with little effort she gave. She barely had any strength left to open the window. When she turned around, she saw him standing there in the middle of the room. She pushed harder against the window and tried to go faster.

"And you thought you'd be able to go. You know what I was going to let you go but you took advantage of me, you took me away, you ripped my heart out and let it fall." He was right behind her and had Billy's heart in his hand and sprinkled some in her hair and let it fall. She shook her head and tried to get it all out, but she couldn't.

"STOP!!" She cried. Tears came down her face.

"Stop!!" She shook her head and didn't want anymore of this she just wanted to go home.

"Tell me what do you really want? Do you want to go home, is that what it is? But I can't let you go home because you tried to hurt me. I can't let you go. I can't do that. It will break my heart. I never had anyone to love. I need you for that. I need you to give me a chance, but you never gave me that chance. Come here," he whispered in her ear. He took her hand and led her the way to an empty room that was clean with a bed that smelled fresh. She stopped crying and let him take her into the room. He gently laid her on the bed.

"I just wanna go home. I just wanna go home," she cried.

"I know, I know. I'll take you home. I'll take you to your home," he whispered in her ear and brought his lips to hers and kissed her gently. He lifted his head up and stared at her and breathed heavily from the kiss.

"Will… yo…" her voice trailed behind and she fell back against the soft bed.

"I'll take you home." He drew his lips heavily toward hers and kissed her once again.

She opened her eyes and saw that he wasn't there. She was able to move around in the small room. The door was closed. She moved toward the door and tried opening it but it was locked. She surveyed the room that was empty except for the bed. There was no window in the room. The walls were covered with wallpaper that might be covering something underneath. There was a little hole in the wall and she moved toward it. Looking through the hole she saw him skin something.

She gasped silently when she saw Heather being taken upstairs. She heard muffled voices at the top and heard the door close. *I thought she was dead. Where are they going? Where are they taking her? What's going on?* Sarah was in a panic. She quickly moved away from the wall when she heard footsteps approaching the room. She stopped in mid stride between the door and the bed. The footsteps continued on and stepped away from the door. Sarah moved ever so silently back toward the wall and looked through the hole again.

She saw someone else moved toward the table that was splattered with blood and a dead body. She saw him rip the skin open and throw it on the floor. She saw him raise a finger and bite a nail off and chew it. She saw that he didn't spit it out, he swallowed it completely. He gathered the body and dispensed it leaving only the skin to play with. Sarah made a disgusting face and gasped. She saw him lift his head up and stare right at her.

She backed away from the wall and fell against the bed. She waited about ten minutes sitting there; scared to death and didn't know what to do. She heard muffled voices from outside the door knowing that someone else was there or he was just talking to himself. She moved ever so quietly toward that wall but not so close that they could see her.

"We have company."

"Who's here?" The other guy just grinned and winked. They both walked away and went upstairs.

Sarah had time to think then, but for some reason she couldn't. She was unable to think right. Her head was still pounding from the sight that she saw and the pain that throbbed continuously in her body. She wanted to leave; she wanted to go home so bad. She turned around and stared at the wall that had no window. Within those minutes she heard noise behind the door. The door finally opened and she breathed in a sigh of relief.

"Don't get so lucky. This is all you get for now," he replied and left and locked the door. Sarah stared at the food that was by the door. She couldn't even look at it. She didn't dare to eat any of it. He probably didn't even watch his hands. Sarah was disgusted from the food and turned away. She tried to sleep only knowing that she wasn't going to be able to sleep at all. She was hungry yet at the same time she wasn't. She wasn't going to eat the food that he gave her. She sat on the bed and cried inside. She crawled under the covers that had a smell to it. She tried to ignore it and tried to sleep.

CHAPTER **16**

There was nothing lurking behind the doors. It was dead silent; the only thing that could be heard was the soft breathing. David stood by the window and watched the stars shine bright except the moon. The moon was never there; it was only the stars. He turned away from the window when he heard Tracy gasp. He walked over to the bed and slipped under the covers.

"Are you okay?"

"Yeah. I had a nightmare that's all. I thought I lost you," she whispered. He looked deep into her eyes that were scared.

"Don't worry. You're not going to lose me. I'm here." He hugged her and held her close.

"Will you be okay now?" She nodded.

"I'm going to go and see Sean and Josh if that's okay." She nodded and lit a smile on her face so that he couldn't see the pain that was hurting her inside. He smiled back but he knew that she was hiding something. He moved back toward the bed.

"I don't wanna see you hurt you know that?"

"I know. I'll be okay." He kissed her lips softly and smiled at her.

"I love you."

"I love you too." As quiet as he could he left. Tracy watched him stand in the doorway making sure that no one was there and made his way to the room across from theirs.

"What the...." He heard Sean reply. Josh jumped up in bed with a knife in his hand.

"Relax. It's just me," David replied. Josh lowered the knife and put a lamp light on. Sean got up from the bed. Sean and David stared at Josh who carried a knife in his hand.

"I took it from the kitchen just in case," he answered before any of them asked him anything.

"Where's Tracy?" Sean was wide awake.

"She's sleeping." There was a moment of silence between them. They couldn't think right then. They just wanted to leave.

"I wish we never came. This stinks," Sean whispered.

"I know."

"I meant the bed." Sean made a small joke but they never laughed. They just smiled thinking and waiting for those happy moments to return, only they won't because of where they were.

"What are we gonna do?" Josh came in. They all sat there in silence whispering their thoughts and ideas of what should happen and what they should do. Finally after fifteen minutes they heard a small groan. They quickly ran to the door and made sure that no one was there and they ran to the other room. They saw that Tracy sleeping fast asleep. They breathed in a sigh of relief knowing that she was okay.

"We're going to go back to our room."

"Stay with us. We need you guys." Tracy moved in her sleep and looked up to find them all standing in the doorway with worried glances on their faces.

"What's wrong?"

"Nothing's wrong." David moved toward the bed and pulled her close to him and kissed the top of her head.

"What's wrong? What's going on?

"Nothing baby. Nothing. There's nothing. I just thought I heard you scream that's all. But you're okay." David soothed her. Sean and Josh moved toward the other bed and sat on top. They all sat there in a moment of silence. They were in desperate need of jokes and laughter and talking with no meaning. They sat there with silence between them until they grew tired and fell asleep.

That night was filled with nothing but sleep. Even though not many of them got enough sleep they whined and complained to each other about how much they missed the good old days. They just wanted those days to come back and fill their dreams with so much. Now, it was nothing. Their dreams were nothing but empty.

Sarah was in deep thought that morning. She stared at the food that was still in her room and watched the food grow cold and stale and hard to chew on. The door rattled and she moved back to the bed. When he came into the room, he saw that she never ate anything.

"What are you doing? Why didn't eat your food?" She didn't say anything.

"Well?"

"I wasn't hungry," her voice was low. She wasn't sure that he heard her.

"You weren't hungry? Is that what you said?" She nodded.

"If you're not going to eat I'll have to tie you back up," he moved toward her with new fresh tape to put on her mouth. She shook her head vigoursly.

"When I come back with food for you, I expect it to be all gone." He moved toward the tray and took it. He closed the door and locked it once again. Sarah was close to tears. She didn't know what to do. She went back to what she was doing. She moved to the other side of the bed and pulled out some things from her pocket. She found a chocolate bar and tried to endure the taste of it.

She also pulled out a pen and her phone. She was happy that she had them with her. She had another chocolate bar yet she didn't want to open it just yet. When she heard the door open, she quickly swallowed the last bite that she took and left her stuff on the floor and moved sat on top of the bed.

"What are you doing?"

"Nothing."

"I better not catch you with anything that I don't wanna see." He moved towards her and gave her the food and set it on the bed beside her. He breathed in a heavy sigh as he moved toward her. The only thing that she could think at that moment was that he would never find out what she was doing. The stale stench of his breath moved closer to her and she tried plugging her nose.

"Mmmm. You still smell good." He left the room and locked it once again. Sarah stared at the food that looked nothing like the same thing that he gave her last night. He knew that he wasn't going to let her go. She also knew that if she didn't eat the food that he gave her and if she didn't do what he wanted, he was going to tie her back up with tape around her. She grabbed the fork that had a small piece of bacon on it. Who knows what he did to the food and what he put in it, Sarah thought.

She moved the fork toward her mouth and it crunched loudly. Sarah gagged when she heard the sound and smelled it. She put the fork down and quickly grabbed the cup of water which only made it worse. She tried to eat some of it only to make him happy. She managed to eat some of the food. While she ate, she plugged her nose so she didn't have to endure it the way he would have wanted her to. The door once again opened.

"Good. You ate it. I thought you would never." He took the tray and left locking the door behind him once again. She breathed in a sigh of relief as he left. She was gagging with the smell and the taste in her mouth. She moved back where she was sitting before and finished eating the chocolate bar. She had another one, but she wanted to save it for later. She took her phone and tried it. There was still no signal. She kept trying until she gave up and fell asleep on top of the bed.

Tracy woke up first and stared out at the window that was barricaded with bars. She watched Sean and Josh kicking each other in the bed that they were sleeping in. Tracy felt the touch of David's arm around her.

"Are you okay?"

"Yeah. It would've been better if the bars weren't there. It would be nicer because of the sun," Tracy smiled.

"Yeah." The sun blared with intensity from its heat. There was nothing else that brightened up the room but their laughter and the heat from the sun that reflected in the room. Sean broke away from Josh's grasp that tightened around him.

"Nightmare?" Tracy smiled.

"No. He was trying to kill me."

"I wouldn't have tried to kill you if you didn't kick me," Josh replied in his sleep. They all laughed. They stopped when they heard footsteps. They grew louder as they came by the room then they grew faint as they left. They all waited for the right moment to talk. Just then they thought they heard the door open to the other room. Their held their breaths waiting for them to open the door to the room they were all in. They didn't dare say anything and waited for the right time to talk. When the footsteps disappeared once again, they breathed in a full sigh of relief.

"We really need to work something out," Sean thought whispering. They all nodded silently in agreement. They all stared at Josh who was still fast asleep. They finally left the room after five minutes and the smell of eggs and bacon and coffee wafted up to the room. They were all hungry, yet at the same time they weren't. They just needed something to eat. They walked into the kitchen to find someone else instead of the guy that introduced them. He turned around and saw them with a bright smile on his face.

"Oh. Well how are our guests? I hope you slept well. I'm sorry we haven't been formally introduced. My brother told me all about you. You all seem uptight. Relax, everything is fine." He looked alike to the other guy, except his features were different. His eyes bulged out like as if he was afraid or something. His lips were thin and were cracked all over. His face wasn't covered with any scratches or marks like the other guy. He had handsome features that made them wonder if he was nicer than the other guy or not.

They lingered in the doorway wondering whether if they should go in or not. But the smell of the food smelled so good. They could hear their stomachs growling from the intensity of the smell.

"Well come on. The table is set and is waiting to fill four hungry stomachs," he replied. As he moved toward the table, he put another bowl on the table that was when Sean noticed a huge knife with blood that stained the whole knife poking from his pocket. He gasped in a short breath of air.

"Is everything okay?" He stood in front of the table waiting for them.

"Uh…. Yeah. Everything's fine," Sean stuttered. They moved to the table slowly keeping them distracted by their thoughts. They finally sat on the table with food filled right to the tops on every corner and the edge so that the table could not be seen from underneath.

"Well. It's all up to you now. I'll leave you to your food," his tongue slithered from his mouth. He grinned before he left. After he left, they all sat there stunned from what they have just seen in the last five minutes. They didn't know what to say.

"I'm hungry," Josh replied after a moment of silence breaking the tension. He grabbed what he thought was a plate instead it was stuffed meat with something poking out of it.

"Never mind." He dropped the plate and turned away.

"What is this anyway?"

"I have no idea." Tracy just stared at the food and looked disgusted. She looked like she was about to throw up.

"It's all heavy meat. Who eats heavy meat in the morning?" Just then the guy came in. It was the other guy who introduced them yesterday and his brother.

"So how are we doing?"

"We can't eat all this."

"Of course you can. It's the best thing that you'll ever eat from here and the best thing that you will ever eat in your entire life." They moved toward the table and quickly sat down and stuffed their mouths with food. Tracy couldn't even look at them. David, Sean, and Josh just stared at them who were well into having their third plate already.

Just watching them, made them gag and wanting to leave as soon as possible. The only things that they ate were some eggs, and the bacon and the toast covered with butter and milk. They waited for the right time to tell them they were finished and wanted to go into their rooms.

"Can we be excused?" Sean asked for them; since he was the only one that did the talking for all of them.

"Of course you can," they replied with their mouths full unable to get a word from their mouths. They quickly left the kitchen and went to the room. Before they left Sean caught a quick glance on the shelf and saw that there was an empty space for a knife and something what looked like an arm with bones poking out and the hand cut off. When they reached the room, they all breathed heavily.

"I don't think my stomach will be able to put up with what it saw," Josh gagged.

"I don't think I'll be able to eat anything for a while," David replied back.

"I don't think I'll be able to think at all," Tracy made faces. They all laughed. Sean didn't say anything. He was lost in his own thoughts.

"Did you see what the guy had in his pocket?"

"No. What was it?"

"He had a huge knife in his pocket that looked like the size of a cutting board or something." They all stared at him in disbelief.

"Did you see what was on the shelf?" David thought aloud. Sean and Josh nodded their heads.

"What. What was it?"

"You really wanna know?" She nodded her head.

"It looked like an arm. The hand was cut off. You can see the bones sticking out and you can tell that it's an arm of an animal or something," Josh told her. Tracy shivered at the thought.

"Don't worry. Nothing's going to happen. Not to us. Not now, not ever," David shook his head.

"Let's just hope that their not what I thought they might be." They all stared at Josh thinking the same thing.

"I highly it doubt it. But for now let's just keep the food in our stomachs and not in our throats." They just knew that they had to figure out what's going on before the time catches them and before they catch them.

CHAPTER 17

Sarah stood in the room trying to think of a way out. She was going to go crazy if he didn't help her. She still wanted to know what happened to Heather. She wanted her to help her out so they could help each other and figure a way out together. But she was gone, they took her somewhere. She whimpered silently in the room.

Her thoughts were interrupted with the sound of the door opening. He came into her room and gave her food without saying a word and locked the door and left. Sarah stared at the food. It was nothing but meat. She managed to eat it by cutting it with a knife before she chewed it, it was no use. She brought it to her mouth and ripped it with her teeth. The meat was hard and it was useless for her to eat it. After twenty minutes he came back.

"Why didn't you eat it?"

"The meat is hard." He slapped her hard across the face. She turned her face back towards him and stared at him. This time she wasn't afraid. She didn't care what he did to her now because she knew she was going to be facing something sooner or later.

"You think I'm hard to fool huh?" He moved away from her and walked to the other side of the bed.

"No." She cried.

"What's this? WHAT'S THIS?" He slapped her again. This time the slap was harder than before and sent her reeling across the room to the wall and she hit her head. He took her phone and the pen and broke them in front of her face. Sarah cried in pain and agony. She lifted her head and saw that the door was wide open. She tried getting up before he got to her and ran out of the room. There was another guy standing outside of the room blocking her way to leave and grabbed her.

"NOOOOOOO." She screamed her loudest so someone could at least hear her.

"Shut up. You know that no one's going to hear you. So shut up." The other guy grabbed the tape and taped her mouth and brought the rope and stuffed her in the room.

"Sweet dreams." They both chuckled, they locked the door and left. Sarah's cries were muffled. She couldn't breathe. The stench from outside the door was getting worse. She was crying inside. She wanted to go home. She looked around her, nothing seemed familiar to her. Soon enough, her eyes started to feel weary and tired. Even though she wasn't tired she tried to keep her eyes open but it was hard for her. Her eyes finally forced themselves shut and her head fell back.

She didn't know where she was. She heard whispers and a low laugh. She tried lifting her head up but it was no use. It felt heavy and her head fell back against something hard.

"You ready?" Sarah heard the low whispers. She finally lifted her head right and opened her eyes. Her eyes grew wider as she saw one of the guys in front of her. The last thing that could be heard from her was her screams. Her screams erupted and ricocheted against the walls and echoed in the elongated narrow room. Long silence erupted and nothing else could be heard. It was dead silent; nothing could be heard, not the sound of any animal scampering and not a sound of screams erupted in the night.

CHAPTER 18

There was nothing left for them to do. They wanted to leave yet at the same time there was something telling them not to. They had to figure a way to get out. If only they could they would be on their way home by now.

"What should we do? Seriously this is really starting to piss me off like very bad," Josh was right on the edge. They were all hanging on the edge waiting for the right time and the right moment. They were more than just upset too because they were not even where they wanted to be.Tracy shivered in the room. Even though heat vibrated in the room, they were all cold.

"Are you okay Tracy?" Sean looked at her.

"Yeah. I'm just cold." She nodded her head with a smile pretending that everything was okay. They all knew nothing was ever going to be okay. David sneaked back into the room from the bathroom and sat next to Tracy. They all breathed in a heavy sigh.

"I have an idea," Josh whispered quietly. He snuck to the door making sure the guys weren't there and motioned them with his hands. They all looked at him wide eyed with horror in their eyes.

"Are you trying to get us killed or something?" Sean looked at him with eyes wider than all of them.

"Come on this will be fun," Josh was already out the door.

"You'll get us killed. Come on get back in before one of them sees you." Josh put a wide grin on his face when he heard footsteps. They closed the door breathing heavily and waited for the footsteps to disappear. When they were clearly gone, they opened the door slowly and quietly making sure it didn't make any noise. When they stared out where Josh stood, he was gone. David closed the door and heavily breathed out before he could talk.

"I'm going to go look for Josh." He stood up ready to leave.

"They probably already found him. Let's just wait and see what happens," Sean pulled him down and they all sat by the door waiting for him.

Josh stood in the hallway and waited for the right time to walk. The floorboards creaked every time he walked. He walked every so slowly and carefully not wanting the guys to see him wandering out of the room. He walked out to the backdoor and saw a small light illuminating from the inside of a small house adjacent to where he stood. He moved closer outside to get a perfect view.

A small smile broke his face.Behind him a figure stood in the doorway to the kitchen. It stood there waiting for him. It stood there for about five minutes watching him, waiting. Finally he left without Josh noticing which followed by a small creak in the floorboards. Josh turned around to see if someone was there.

"Hello?" There was nobody there except for him. He went back to where he stood and made out a small figure out in the distance. Josh moved away so that he couldn't be seen. Another figure stood behind him and waited for him this time. When Josh turned around, he jumped when he saw Sean standing there.

"Oh fuck man. You scared me half to death," Josh rested his hand on his chest.

"What are you doing? They could catch you man."

"Shhhh," Josh silenced him as they heard footsteps coming toward them. They didn't know where to hide. They ran from the backdoor to the kitchen where the footsteps were coming from. They knew that one of them had to hide. The footsteps got louder and louder. The floorboards creaked louder and louder each time along with the footsteps. Sean looked around for a place to hide, knowing that there was no other place he hid under the table. Josh stood in the kitchen waiting for the footsteps to stop. The light was turned on and Josh squinted in the dimness of the light.

"Are you okay?" Sean heard someone in the kitchen he knew it was one of the guys.

"Oh, uh, yeah. I was just getting a glass of water. I, uh, wasn't sure where you kept the cups," Josh stuttered. He hoped that he didn't catch it. Sean shut his eyes tight not wanting Josh to say something stupid. He heard the footsteps going somewhere else and coming back into the kitchen.

"Does this happen often?" Sean heard them mutter a couple of words in the dimly lit kitchen.

"Sometimes. When I'm awake I tend to drink a lot of water even before I go to bed." Sean was starting to get cramped up under the table. He wasn't sure if he could hold it anymore. His eyes started to water and perspiration started. He couldn't wait anymore. The light that was on was shut off. He heard the footsteps leave and he breathed in a sigh of relief. Another set of footsteps was still in the kitchen. It moved toward the table where he heard noise.

It breathed heavily and stood there for about five minutes. Sean heard them put something on the table and scrape a knife against something. He breathed in a small heavy gasp and waited for him to leave. When he didn't leave, he knew that he was in for it. He had a feeling that who ever was in there was never going to leave. He heard other footsteps coming in the kitchen and stood before the table and heard low whispers.

"What are we going to do with this?"

"I don't know ask him."

"We'll cut this in half and then cut it in quarters and then cut it into smaller pieces." Sean was starting to perspire a lot. He waited for them to leave. Sean was about to give up when they heard them talk about Josh.

"Next time he does that again we'll just let him have it. Serves him right." Sean heard them chuckle so low that it almost made him throw up.

"Oops." One of them dropped a knife and reached down to pick it up. Sean noticed blood on the knife. It was the same knife that he saw before and it made him want to throw up really bad. After almost ten minutes he heard them leave. He waited another couple of minutes under the table making sure they were completely gone. Sean quietly revealed himself from under the table and as slowly and quietly as he could, he ran from the kitchen and upstairs.

It was then he realized that he was not in the right place. It was darker then before and it was damp. There was only four rooms rather than six. There was no light illuminating anywhere. He heard low guttering sounds and saw a light coming from a room. He moved towards it and saw two guys sitting on the bed with someone else and made slurping noises and moaned heavily. Sean gasped and he went wide-eyed. The noises stopped and turned toward the door.

He quickly found another room and hid in it until they were gone. He heard the door close tight to the other room. Sean quickly fled the room and ran downstairs and went up another set of staircase and recognized it almost instantly because of one of the doors was slightly ajar with light while the others were closed tight. He quickly moved toward the room not caring if he made any noise at all. He just wanted to get back. He moved toward the room and closed it tight and made sure it was shut tight. Josh David and Tracy sat on the bed waiting for him.

"Where were you? I was looking all over for you," Josh whispered heavily.

"I was still hiding under the table and I thought I heard someone in the kitchen and I thought it was you but it was those guys. I waited under the table for almost twenty minutes. W hen they did leave, I was coming upstairs but I realized that I went up different stairs and I saw something that made me almost throw up," Sean gasped heavily and hoarsely. He fell against the door and tried to get his breathing right. It only got worse and he had to reach for his inhaler to help him relax better. They all stared at Sean that made them think that something or someone is out there and they are just waiting for them and for the right moment to kill them.

"What was it that you saw?"

"I don't think that any of you want to know. It was very disgusting and it made me want to throw up very bad," Sean moved toward the bed after he got his breathing right and he was able to walk. They all sat on one bed thinking the same thing, yet at the same time they weren't sure about it.

"You know what; I regret everything that I said about Billy. I don't think that he is not even in this at all." Josh was starting to think that he had something.

"What are you thinking? Of course Billy had to do with everything that we thought."

You were the one who thought of it first." Sean whispered back.

"I saw Billy a couple of days ago."

"Here?" Sean replied heavily. He brought his inhaler back to his mouth when his breathing became rapid. Josh nodded. They were all wide-eyed and didn't expect to hear Josh say that.

"I was going to get a drink of water and I heard noise and I hid under the table and I saw them bring someone in. And I could tell that it was Billy because of the pants he wore and his hands. They took him to this one house outside and I saw them take off the mask and pat him on the back or something. And they put the mask back on him. I don't know that's what I saw." They were all quiet for a moment. There was nothing that seemed right for them not since they came into the house.

CHAPTER 19

It was lifeless in the house. It was never disturbed in the night and never in the morning. There was nothing to do now that they were well into being afraid. They still sat on top of the bed trying to figure out what they were going to do. They tried making up their minds debating whether they should stay one more night. It wasn't their idea of being stranded in the middle of nowhere and getting lost and finding their way into a house and being lured in without permission. They forgot all about going to Darwin since they got lost and stranded in the middle of nowhere. Right now all they wanted was to go home.

The day drifted by slow. They weren't sure if they wanted to eat supper that night. They ate the same thing everyday and they had enough of it. The heat got worse in the room. They tried to open the windows, but they were barred like they were in prison. They tried making up plans how to escape but they had nothing to think of.

That night while Josh went to get a drink of water, Sean, David, and Tracy left the room to find something that would get them to leave. As Josh went to get a drink of water, something caught his attention. He moved toward the back door away from the kitchen and saw a dim light illuminating from the other house. He looked back inside the house making sure that no one was there and left.

He walked ever so slowly away from the house. He looked back to find that he was ten feet away. He breathed in heavily and walked forward. He drifted like a ghost in the darkness of the night. When he was close to the house, he found it to be a garage as he opened the door slowly. He jumped when he heard a low hum coming from behind him. He turned around only to see that it was the furnace going on. His eyebrows drew in as he wondered why the furnace was on when it was already hot enough. When he moved in closer he realized why it was on.

It grew colder as he went in deeper. His teeth chattered against each other like a skeleton clapping against the wall. He stopped in mid stride when he heard diminutive undertones. He didn't want to budge any longer. He thought that if he did, he would get caught. As slow and calm as he could, Josh moved his body toward the staircase and descended with caution. A tiny moan from a room disrupted his thoughts as he was completely downstairs. He didn't have enough time to look around him. He moved toward the room and tried to open one of the doors it was locked. He moved to another one and also found it locked.

He moved to a room at the end. He tried the knob and it opened. He opened it slowly and stared right through. He gasped when he saw Sarah lying in a bed with blood pouring from her mouth. Her tongue was cut in half, and her teeth ripped out. Josh moved into the room and sat on the bed. He cried softly and grabbed her hand. When he did, her arm fell off. Josh jumped from the bed and stared at her. Tears were streaming down his face that he hadn't realized it. He wanted to know what happened. Josh was scared and shaking that he hadn't heard a low gruff behind him. He turned around to see someone behind him.

"Y…Y…You d…did this?" Josh couldn't get the words from his mouth. He was shaking.

"Maybe." He smiled a wide grin that showed his teeth. Josh stared back at Sarah. Josh had the nerve had to kill him. He moved toward him and jumped on top of him and punched him hard. He was stronger than Josh. He pushed Josh off and punched him back. Josh caught his arm and stopped he realized that it was the same guy that attacked Tracy.

"NOO." Josh pushed him off of him and ran back upstairs and out of the place. He panted heavily as he ran away from the garage. He stopped and stared back to see if he was following him. He turned back around to see someone else in front of him. He ran toward Josh and pushed him on the ground and fought with him. Josh struggled with him. He was in a tight situation. He heard other footsteps coming toward him. In less than a minute he felt everything go black and he drifted into a heavy sleep.

"Where's Josh?" Tracy thought aloud.

"He went to get water remember?" Sean turned toward her.

"This is no use man," David cried from inside the room. He walked out of the room.

"It's no use. There's nothing. Either the windows are locked and barred or there are no windows." In the distance they heard shouts and screams. They ignored it knowing that it was probably an animal or something.

"You guys have to come see this." They heard Sean in another direction. They ran towards where he was and went up another different flight of stairs.

"Come on." He beckoned them towards a room that was slightly ajar. They walked slowly.

"What is it?" When they reached the room, they gasped as they saw something on top of the bed. Tracy turned away and gasped heavily. Sean walked in the room and tried to figure out what it was. He came back out and looked at them with a look that said there was something really going on.

"What is it?" David asked.

"It's Heather."

"What?" David went into the room and walked back out with a disgusted look on his face. She was sprawled out on top of the bed. Her body was limp and blood pooled around her. Her head was facing toward the door and her eyes were wide open. Her eyes were empty, almost glass-like. And her stomach had been opened; empty like the rest of her.

"What do you think happened?" David said after a moment of silence.

"I don't know but there's a chance that something or someone killed her or something." The three of them stood there for a while thinking and wondering what they were going to do. Their eyes grew wide as they heard noise from the kitchen. They couldn't go back downstairs, the kitchen was right across and they would see them. They tried the first room but it was locked. They moved to another from across it was also locked. Sean moved to the last room at the end of the hall and the door opened.

"Come on," Sean whispered. They quietly ran to the end of the hall and closed the door behind them as they were inside. They stared at each other with the same thing going on in their minds. They heard shuffling noises in the hallway. It moved toward the room but opened another door instead and locked it behind them. They heard muffled voices in the room. Tracy shivered and her body shook as small tears form under her eyelids.

"Shhhh. We can't let them hear us," Sean whispered. They sat there still and quiet waiting for the right time. When they heard the door slam shut from across of the other room, David, ever so slowly, opened the door and saw that all the doors were closed especially the door to the room where they saw Heather. David got up and took Tracy's hand.

"What are you doing?" Sean's voice took on a surprising tone even though he was whispering.

"Come on. We have to leave now." David and Tracy left the room with Sean behind them as he closed the door. They walked slowly down the stairs as they creaked. David and Tracy moved toward the back of the kitchen to the door.

"What are you doing?"

"We have to leave."

"They'll find out. And they'll kill us."

"I'm not going to risk that. Besides we need to leave. This isn't our place. We weren't even invited. But they think we are. We need to find our place and it's not here." They heard a banging noise from upstairs.

"I was almost killed. Did you forget that?"

"We need to leave before one of us is next."

"Where's Josh?" Tracy asked once again. He wasn't in the kitchen. They were supposed to meet in the kitchen but he wasn't there.

"He probably went back to the room."

"If he did it would've took him only five minutes he wouldn't take forever," David replied back.

"I'll go check." Sean left the kitchen and went upstairs. He saw the light still illuminating in the room.

He thought that maybe Josh forgot that he had to wait downstairs. He knocked at the door.

"Hey Josh. What's wrong? I…." When he opened the door he saw a figure standing in the room.

"Come on man. Quit playing tricks we need to leave. David and Tracy are waiting downstairs." His voice shook. His body shook with nervousness.

"Josh?" He heard footsteps behind him thinking that it was David and Tracy. But he didn't have enough time to turn around. A scream erupted from his mouth.

"What was that?" Tracy cried.

"Come on." David held her hand tightly against his. They ran upstairs to look for Sean and Josh.

"Sean where are you." They moved toward the room. He wasn't there. Tracy moved to David.

"What if they got him like they got Josh?"

"I don't think they did."

"But what if they did?" That was a question that David could not answer. They went deeper in the room and got their stuff from the room. David saw Sean's and Josh's bag against the other bed.

"They're still here." He pointed to their stuff. They heard banging noises coming from downstairs. Tracy gasped.

"Come on." They moved to the doorway to find no one there. They ambled quietly near the staircase not daring each other to go downstairs.. They saw Sean stumble in the darkness. Tracy was about to move toward him but David kept her close to him. Sean ran up to them.

"We have to go back to the room. We have to go back." There was no lock on the door to lock it. Sean tried pushing one of the dressers toward the door. David quickly helped him and drew it against the door and Sean slumped against it with his inhaler in his mouth.

"Whatever that thing is or was, went after Josh and is coming after us," Sean breathed when he got his breathing steady once again. David held onto Tracy and didn't let go. David stared at Sean and they both had the same idea going on in their heads. Tracy fell asleep in David's arms. He gently laid her back in bed and sat back on top of the bed. He sighed heavily and put his head in his hands.

"What are we going to do?" David wondered a loud in a heavy whisper.

"There's nothing that we can do. I wish I was home right now. If mom ever found out she would've took us out."

"Why do you always have to bring mom in a situation like this? You know she's not here and if she was, god help us please. I would never want to see her here. I don't ever want to see anybody lay a hand on her." They were silent for a moment. They heard noise from across the hall. They sat on the same bed while the noise disappeared and faded.

<h1>CHAPTER 20</h1>

It was a slow night for them. David and Sean sat on one bed trying to put in their heads what just happened in the last couple of hours; which to them seemed more than just a couple of hours. David stared at Tracy who slept peacefully. A small smile formed on his face as he watched her sleep. He made a fist and covered his mouth so he wouldn't cry. Tears formed under his eyelids as he covered his cries with one hand. He fell away from the bed and walked toward the window and gave a heavy sigh. He turned to Sean who was ready to sleep.

"Sean. Sean are you sleeping?"

"No." He mumbled.

"I lied."

"What?"

"I lied about what I told you before."

"About what?" He moaned with sleep in his eyes.

"About mom." Sean lifted his body away from the bed and sat on top of the bed.

"What about mom?"

"You know how the other day I told you that mom kicked me out, and there was those two guys"

"Yeah. What about it?"

"Before mom kicked me out she told me that…. Never mind." He moved away from the bed

"What? What did she tell you?" Sean got up from the bed and walked to the window. They stared at Tracy who moved in her sleep.

"Never mind. I don't know why I brought it up."

"Come on tell me. I'm already mad as it is. Nothing really is gonna help anyways. Might as well get the worst out of this." David sighed heavily and his eyes watered with tears. He didn't even want to say it anymore.

"What's wrong?" David looked at him and shook his head. A noise erupted from the hallway. Tracy woke up with a jolt. They all gathered close together as the door was trying to push open. There was no place for them to hide. They moved away from the window.

"Come on Tracy." Tracy got up and grabbed David's hand. They had no where to go.

"Come on." Sean was already beckoning them toward the closet. David and Tracy walked silently and quickly toward the closet and he closed it. The door finally opened all the way. They heard someone gasp heavily and call someone else.

"What?"

"They're not here."

"What are you talking about? This can't be right. What if they left?" He stared at the window.

"They can't leave. All the windows are barred and I just put an alarm."

"But there's only one window on this wing that's not locked."

"But the door is locked also."

"Find them." They heard them in a deep discussion. They stood in the closet waiting to leave. Sean's foot was getting numb and he shuffled his foot on something and he stopped knowing that they might have heard the noise.

"What was that?"

"What?"

"Listen…" Sean, David and Tracy didn't dare to move another muscle. They couldn't hold it anymore. They didn't know exactly how long they waited in the closet; they just wanted them to leave. Finally after what seemed like forever, they left. David gasped as he jumped out of the closet and grabbed a hold of Tracy's hand in his as she got out.

Sean quickly grabbed his inhaler as he got out. Just as was looking for it, he couldn't find it.

"What's wrong?" David looked at him.

"My inhaler, it's gone."

"Did you check over there?" He pointed to the dresser that was pushed away from the door. Everything was piled on the floor in a big heap of mess.

"I checked everywhere." David and Tracy helped Sean look for his inhaler. They couldn't find it. They looked everywhere. The room was already upside down and it was no use to find anything in it.

"What are we going to do with Josh's bag?"

"We'll take it with us."

"Hey guys you have to come and see this." They moved to where Sean was. He was in the closet.

"What are you doing in there?" David looked in and he wasn't there.

"Where are you?" Sean jumped up and scared them and laughed.

"That wasn't funny you know."

"What are you doing?"

"There's another room in here." David held tight on to Tracy's hand and they made their way in the closet and in to the other room. The room was smaller than the other. It was much neater than the other one. There was no window in the room. There was no other furniture in the room except for the bed.

"What if they come back?" Tracy's voice shivered.

"They won't know that we're in here."

"How do you know?" David turned to Sean.

"There's a door so they won't find us. And we can lock it." Sean went toward the door and locked it.

"Why wasn't it locked before?"

"I unlocked it."

"How?" Sean lifted two bobby pins in his hands.

"Hey those are mine."

"Too bad," Sean laughed. David laughed at them both. That was the first time they laughed since they were there.

"I'll be right back."

"Where are you going?"

"I'm just going to get the rest of the stuff. Don't worry, I'll be okay." David kissed her cheek.

"I don't know if I'll be able to sleep in one bed with you two."

"Then don't," David replied as he was back in the room with the three bags in his hands. Sean quickly went to the closet and closed the door and locked it.

"What if they heard us?" Tracy whispered softly.

"I don't think they did. What's wrong with you? I thought you always light things up for us?"

"That was before all this happened. I don't think I even want to go on a trip anymore."

"Not even England?"

"Not even England." David laughed at them.

"I think it's time for some of us to get some sleep."

"Yeah I don't think I'll be able to sleep at all."

"Then don't. You can sleep in the other room if it bothers you."

"Hell no." They laughed at each other. Tracy got herself to sleep in seconds. While she was fast asleep, David moved toward the window where Sean stood. David sighed heavily.

"I think we had enough of all this. I can't stand this anymore." David leaned against the window and watched Tracy with a smile on the corner of his mouth.

"You know how before you were going to tell me something about mom?" David hung his head and gave another sigh. He lifted his head and stared at Sean. David got right to it.

"You know how mom said we don't have a dad? Well guess what? We do" Sean's eyes grew wider. "When did she tell you this?"

"She didn't tell me as much as I "found" out."

"Wow."

"I know hey? It's crazy how stuff like this happens."

"I know." They both sighed heavily.

"Aren't you going to bed?"

"Nah. I'm just….I don't know. So much has happened. I don't think I'll be able to sleep anyways." They both sat on the floor by the window and tried to think of something else.

"I remember one time me and dad went to the hospital to see mom. And I guess I wondered off and I didn't know where I was and there was this room with this really old lady who kind of looked like somebody that I know I think. And I heard dad call me. He found me standing in the middle of the hallway in front of her. And we walked away and dad wiped a tear from my eyes because I thought maybe it was someone else.

"Anyways we went back whatever. And that was when dad and I saw these guys going in to the room where mom was and he like ran right after them in to the room. And mom didn't say or do anything. Dad got mad. He yelled at them. "If you ever come near my family, I swear to god I will kill you." Everybody could hear everything. The whole entire floor was right out the door. It was crazy."

"What did he do?"

"Nothing. He couldn't do anything. He didn't want to start something so we just left."

"That was when I was born right?"

"Yeah. And mom was smoking right in front of you and holding you at the same time and the doctors and nurses tried to make her stop. But those guys were there, so nobody really couldn't do anything."

"Wow. I kind of missed those days where we were able actually to do something."

"Yeah. After dad got custody of me and mom got custody of you, there was nothing that we were able to do."

"Yeah. I wish none of that wouldn't have happened. I remember that was about almost five years ago when mom told me about you."

"Yeah and five years after that we're still going." They were silent and were slumped against the wall with a bottle in their hands.

"You still got those bobby pins?" Sean and David walked toward the door. Sean tried to unlock the door until he heard it click. He opened the door quietly and slowly. They looked over to Tracy who was still fast asleep. They left the room quietly and looked around. Sean went deeper into the hallway and made sure that no one was there.

Sean opened the door across from them and saw that the window was barred. He cursed under his breath as he walked out of the room. He went to the next room and unlocked it. He stared around the room there was no window. There was no use. He wanted to find the room that had the opened window. There were two rooms left. He opened both and found that the last room had the opened window. Just then, he heard noise coming from near by the stairs.

"Hurry up Sean?" He heard David whisper. Sean quickly went to the other rooms making sure that they were locked and ran back to the room and locked it. He slumped against the door.

"I found the room." He dragged himself away from the door to the bed. They were quiet for a moment. That was when they heard noise from the other room.

CHAPTER 21

"**F**IND THEM." He heard one of them scream.

"We have to get out."

"Tracy come on wake up. We have to leave." David lightly pushed Tracy and held on to her hand.

"What's going on?" She woke up. They moved to the door and waited for the right time to leave as Sean opened the door. Making sure that no one was there, Sean quickly led them the way to the room. He couldn't open it. Last time when he tried it opened, this time it wouldn't open. He pushed himself against the door and tried to open it. The door wouldn't budge.

They heard noise coming back up the stairs. Sean tried it again. He was about to give up when the door finally opened. They ran into the room and locked the door behind them. David ran to the window and it opened without any difficulty. David went first along with Tracy. Sean was the last one to get out. He made sure the door was locked and ran to the window and closed it tight making sure it was closed. They all stood on the ledge of the window. David looked down and saw that there was nothing for them to land on.

"I'm scared," Tracy whispered heavily. David turned around the corner of the ledge where the jump was low enough to land and jumped off, Tracy followed but didn't jump.

"Don't worry."

"What if I fall?"

"You won't fall. I'll catch you." Tracy closed her eyes tight hoping that none of this wasn't happening. When she opened her eyes, she found herself still standing on the ledge. She closed her eyes once more and let herself fall and David caught her.

"Told you I'd catch you," David replied with a small on his face. Tracy smiled back. Sean was the last one on the ledge.

"Hurry up Sean. I think they're coming." They heard noise coming from somewhere but they didn't know exactly where. Sean quickly jumped off and the three of them stood there waiting. Sean walked away; David and Tracy followed suit. They had no idea where they were going; they just knew that they had to get out of there.

They walked into the garage hiding away from them. Sean stood by the door with Tracy beside him. They walked so slowly away from the door and walked down the stairs that creaked with every step they took. David was behind them walking slowly. He was last to reach the bottom of the landing of the stairs. They breathed in a heavy sigh of relief, glad they lost them. The one thing that they didn't know was where they were. Just as long as they lost them, they didn't care about anything else. They walked silently across the floorboards that creaked louder than ever every time they walked.

"What are we exactly doing here?" Sean answered in the dark.

"I have no idea," David whispered back. They tried looking for lights to turn some on, there was none. Sean clicked on a string that hung over a table. A dim light lit up the room. There was a stench that got their attention. They plugged their noise afraid of the stench and afraid of throwing up. The floor was filled with blood dripping from everywhere. Bare skin of some animal hung on a line, the organs were scattered on the table.

The stench grew stronger and it was difficult for them to hold their noses any longer. Their eyes moved around. They saw chains against a pole; a heavy mattress was off to the side covered with blood or what looked like it. David held on to Tracy's hand as they walked around. Sean walked into a room that was empty with no furniture in the room. He walked into another place. He thought it was the kitchen.

He walked deeper and saw fingers of some kind of animal or human in the sink, soaking in cold water.

He covered his mouth. He walked out and tried to ignore what he just saw. They were silent for a moment with no words between them. A noise from behind them interrupted their thoughts. They huddled against each other hoping that it wasn't them. The noise was coming from one of the rooms. Sean moved forward wanting to know what it was.

"Sean get back." He turned around toward David and Tracy and turned back and walked with caution. He reached the door and tried to open it. Just as he thought, it was locked and he tried to open it with the bobby pins. The noise from behind the door stopped. Just as the door clicked open, the bobby pins broke in half.

"Damn it," He swore under his breath. Half of the bobby pins were stuck in the doorknob. He tried taking them out but it was no use. He forgot about the bobby pins and opened the door half way. There was something across the room that caught his attention. He turned to David and Tracy wide – eyed. He turned back and opened the door all the way. He walked into the room. David held onto Tracy hoping that it was nothing bad that would make them regret.

"What the hell man?" They heard loud voices coming from the room. They saw Sean coming from the room along with Josh.

"What happened to you?" David was shocked to see him.

"We thought you were dead." Sean followed. They didn't give him a minute to catch his breath. He pointed to the two doors beside the one he was in. Sean and Josh walked toward the doors they were both unlocked. One of them rooms had a great stench that filled up the rest of the place. The other room was filled with saws and knives hung on the wall and heads of animals and heads from something else as trophies. They backed away from the rooms.

"What happened?" David asked again.

"I was getting a drink of water and whatever and I went outside 'cause I thought I saw a cop or someone, and I wanted to tell them. So I came in here 'cause I saw them come in here. And the next thing I knew everything went black." They were in a lull for more than a while. Banging noise came from upstairs. They turned around and looked at each other trying to figure something out. Josh went in another direction and hid behind something.

"Over here. Hurry up." They quickly made their way to where he was and stood there in silence with no movement and no breathing coming from them.

"I want them. Hurry up and find them. I don't care if anything happens. Just hurry up and find them and take care of them before I take care of you." One of them left and spoke under his breath.

"What did you say?" He angered his voice.

"Nothing." He left without a single word.

They stood behind a long and wide pole that covered them and their bodies so that none of the guys could see them. Sean's and Josh's eyes went wide. They both had the same idea in mind: The room. More noise was erupted and they were about to think of something.

"He's gone."

"WHAT?" They were in shock and panic. Josh was about to leave.

"What are you doing?" Josh put his finger to his mouth and kept going. Sean followed him. They stood beside each other. They had their backs to them facing the table and doing something. The other guy was gone. Josh went first with a knife in his hand and Sean followed him suit. Josh made his way behind the guy. Without making any noise, he wrapped his arm around him with his other hand holding a knife and stabbed him.

He dragged the knife right out of him and took a paper towel and cleaned the knife. They went back when they heard the other guy coming from a different direction. Sean still stood there waiting. Josh beckoned him to hurry up.

"What do you want me to...." The other guy came back. His voice trailed along as he saw him standing there.

"Don't worry about anything. Just go and find them." Sean stood behind the guy holding him and mimicking his voice with his head down playing around with the skin.

"Are you sure? Do you want me to...."

"GO." He left and made sure he heard him leave. Sean threw the guys dead body on the ground. Josh stared at him with shock and amazement in his eyes.

"What happened?" David and Tracy stood behind them.

"We have to hurry up come on." Not a word was said until they were upstairs. Sean ran back downstairs.

"Where are you going?"

"My inhaler." He saw his inhaler on the table. Just as he was about to grab his inhaler, one of the guys got to it first.

"And you thought I was hard to fool." He brought his hand and slapped him across the face hard. Sean reeled back, but that didn't stop him from hitting him back. Sean pushed him back and he landed on the table and the table fell. Josh, David, and Tracy ran downstairs watching Sean struggle in the fight. The guy grabbed a knife from the floor and stabbed him in the arm.

"Josh take David and Tracy out of here," He struck him again.

"NOW." David held onto Tracy's hand and quickly left. Josh stayed behind with Sean. The other guy came from behind him and they both struggled. There was nothing for them to do but fight them with little hope. He pushed Josh against the wall and choked him. His face was turning purple. With all of his strength he pushed him off and pushed him into a room and locked it.

He moved toward Sean and helped him. He pushed the guy on his feet and let Sean do the rest. Sean pushed him against the wall. He stared in the other room that was filled with knives. His eyes grew wide with amazement as he stared at the walls and the table that overlapped the room with knives and all different sorts of knives.

He pushed him in the room and threw him heavily against the wall. His body went limp against the wall. His body hung against the wall like a cross. Both Sean and Josh were tired. They stared at each other with their thoughts twisting in different directions. Sean walked over the table that was tipped over with the skin and a dead body on the floor. He grabbed his inhaler and breathed slowly. Noise from upstairs brought their attention. David came running downstairs with Tracy behind him.

"What are you doing?"

"Thought you might need some help." He held two jugs of oil in his hands.

"Where did you get those?"

"Behind the garage." Josh ran upstairs and left the door behind him open. David stood waiting for Josh. When he came back, the two of them spilled the jugs around. Josh spilled half of it by one of the rooms where the last guy was. They spilled it around until they were upstairs by the door and there was no where for them to go but outside. David lit up a match and threw it and they all watched the flames grow higher and burn what was left of the place. Smoke started to build up higher and none of them could breathe. They quickly went outside where they breathed in a heavy breath of fresh air.

EPILOGUE

Not a word was said to one another as they left. There was nothing for them to say. They all had a hard time. They all sat in the back except for Sean who had to sit in the front because there was no more room in the back for him. Josh was already fast asleep and so were David and Tracy.

They each woke up one by one as they heard sirens and noises around them. They found themselves each by their houses. Josh left first along with David and Tracy. The one thing that Sean was not looking forward to was going home. He didn't want to go home and find his mom not there. He felt empty inside and there was nothing for him to do but wait for what was going to happen next.

When he did get home, there was a car in the driveway waiting for him. His head hung low as he walked the rest of the way to the house.

"What else was I supposed to do?" He heard his mom. He stared at the car and stared back at the house. He thought that there was someone else that he might or might not know that was with his mom. They both stopped talking when they saw him come in. The guy stared at him with a smile Sean ignored his mom and turned and left.

"What's wrong with him?" He heard him reply.

"What do you mean 'what's wrong with him?'" He heard them argue once again. He fell on top of his bed with nothing to think about except the fact that he was happy that he was home. He just didn't want anything else to happen. He felt his phone vibrate in his pocket.

"Hello."

"What's up man?" David sounded pretty perked.

"Not much. I'm just fuckin' happy to be home right now."

"Yeah. That's the best thing that happened for us." They were silent for a moment. They both heard the screaming from downstairs.

"What's that?"

"I don't know. Mom and someone are in a fight." Just then there was a knock on his door.

"Can I come in?" He heard the guy from the other side of the door.

"I'll call you later."

"Sure. No problem. I'm kinda in a mess anyways." They both laughed. The door opened half way and his head peeked in.

"Am I interrupting anything?" "Uh, no. No."

"Why did ignore your mother like that?"

"Is that any of your business?"

"Yes it is."

"There's nothing I can do anyways," Sean walked away from his bed and went over to his desk.

"What's that supposed to mean?"

"What's any of it supposed to mean? Look I'm in a tight situation here and there's nothing I can do with her doing things that I'm hoping that she will regret. That's all I can say okay. What more do you want from me?" Sean cried.

"Nothing. I just thought that maybe taking your mom out of jail and buying you and David a car would satisfy anything." That made Sean think back what he said to him. He wanted to take back those things he said to him.

"All I ever wanted was for you and your mom to be happy. But she took advantage of that. We were actually discussing the things that she had done. The way you reacted to all of it, and the way you made her proud."

"How did I ever make her proud? She was drunk in everyway. She was never proud of me anyways," Sean scoffed.

"Just listen to me okay. You were the last thing on my mind when we were in the hospital and you still are."

"What about David?"

"What about him?"

"Was he the first thing on your mind when he was born?"

"There's nothing in the world that made us happy than what we were before. And we still are. But there's no reason why you can't make your mother proud of you, starting now." He stared at him. They both sat on top of the bed with his arm around him. Sean left the room with no words to say to him.

"Mom?" He walked into the kitchen and saw her sitting by the table drinking a cup of coffee. He sat down beside her and took her hands but she shrugged her hands away from him. He turned around to find his dad standing there in the middle of the kitchen with a frown on his face.

"That's the one thing I can't do," he said to him before he left. Sean sat on the staircase outside. He heard him come out with nothing being said to one another. Sean walked over to the car that stood in the driveway waiting for him. He traced his fingers around it. The car looked like a spider to him. He traced his fingers on the open door and went inside. He noticed that there was more than what a car would have.

"I added some new things to it." He stared at him through the window. Sean tried a button that opened the hood. It was more than what he wanted. It was nothing compared to the other cars that had half parts or broken parts that costed an arm and a leg to pay for them.

"You like it?" Sean got out of the car and overlooked it once again and nodded.

"Thanks." He smiled at him.

"I don't think David recognized the car in the driveway."

"He doesn't recognize things right away. It takes him years. At least a week maybe." They both laughed. That was the first time that Sean met his dad after some years back. He saw his mom standing in the doorway watching him admire the car. Sean watched him walk over to her and took her hands. They walked towards the car and he said something to her that made her smile. A small tear formed under Sean's eyes. He walked over to his mom and took her hands. This time she let him. She hugged him close which surprised him.

"I'm proud of you," she whispered in his ear. Sean stared at him and he nodded with a smile.

"Why don't we take it for a spin? We'll show it off to David." His dad came up to him.

"I don't think he'll notice."

"Why not? His car is different from yours. His car has the same features. The only difference is the colour of the car and the colour of this car is better."

"He's probably busy anyways."

"Doing what?"

"Never mind," Sean thought that it was a mistake for him saying that. He got in the front of the drivers seat.

"I'm driving actually," his dad called.

"I thought it was my car?" Sean caught him. They all laughed as they got in the car with Sean driving and his mom in the front and his dad in the back.

"Easy on the wheels. You can't get the right type of wheels from here. And the rims, you sure and the hell can't get them from here." Sean laughed.

"I think I'll be okay." He turned in where David was. He stopped by the driveway and honked the horn. He laughed quietly to himself. He felt happy inside.

"What?" He heard him scream. He saw David lean over the window and stared down. He saw Sean stand out from the car and beckoning him to come out. They could hear the front door open and slam shut.

"What's this? You got it from eBay or something?" He laughed with food in his mouth.

"You're funny."

"I know I am. It's in my genes." Sean mocked his laughter. David turned around and his eyes grew wide.

"What's that car doing in my driveway? I thought I parked my car here. That's not my car man." Sean laughed at David who took forever to realize the car in his driveway.

"Holy shit man. This car's got like millions of buttons in it." He tried one of the buttons which opened the hood.

"What the hell?" Sean couldn't help but laugh at him. David turned around and stared at him.

"What's so funny? This car is like ET or something." Just then the guy in the backseat got out and watched him admire it. David's eyes grew wide.

"That's what I get from you?" His dad replied.

"No I have worse ideas of what I think about this car. What happened to my other car?"

"I traded it in."

"What. Why?" David shouted.

"It doesn't suit you."

"Hey that car was the best car ever. I even named it."

"What did you name it?" Sean replied between the laughter.

"Quit laughing at me you don't have the right to laugh at me." He pointed his finger toward Sean. His mom also got out and walked over to David. David was in shock at what was happening all at once. Both Sean and David hid something between each other that only they did not even want to know about it, especially talk about it. There was something about that day that made Sean and David realize that something might happen.

The moon peeked through the sky among the stars that shone brighter than before as if they were glad that the moon reappeared back in the sky. The sky was an overcast colour with the moon and the stars shining as small heavy clouds appeared.

"So what do you think?" Sean asked.

"I'm going to kill myself if it's not the last thing I do. I'm hoping nothing has happened between them yet." David grimaced.

"No you freak. I meant about the car."

"Oh the car. Yeah it's nice. I thought you were talking about something else. I like it. Who knew that dad would ever do that." David stopped talking.

"What did you think I was talking about?"

"I thought you were talking about mom and dad."

They both stopped walking thinking that they went far enough. They turned back around.

"I just hope that they didn't do anything to my house."

"Yeah. They're probably doing something." Sean laughed at him. David stopped and punched his arm.

"Ow. What was that for?"

"I just felt like punching you. It makes me feel good." Sean punched him back.

"Ow. I didn't punch you that hard."

"Yeah well your hand rested on my arm for like five seconds."

"Yeah right." David punched him back. Sean grabbed his arm and twisted it.

"Say mercy." He twisted his hand.

"Okay okay. Stop." He let go of his arm and David punched him hard once again.

"That's the fricken third time."

"Yeah well deal with it."

"It's hard for me to deal with your screaming."

"Yeah and it's hard for me to deal with your sleepwalking and hear you talk in your sleep." He laughed.

"I never sleepwalk and I don't talk in my sleep."

"Yeah right. I have it videotaped." He showed him his phone. He laughed hard.

"Give me that." They struggled and fought with each other. They stopped fooling around when a car passed by them slowly.

"Well look who it is." They shook their heads and walked off and ignored them.

"I hope you enjoyed your trip escaping jail." David looked at him. A police car stopped right behind him from its distance that it kept from him.

"You'll regret this day I swear to god you will. I'm going to kill you so you better watch." They watched him being taken away once again.

"I don't know how many times I hear his voice in my sleep. It's like a frickin' bee or something. I just wanna kill it." Sean hung his head low.

"I don't even want to go in there anymore." They stood by the curb staring at the house.

"Why?"

"I don't know. I just don't want to go in there."

"Why? Because mom and dad are in there?" David punched him.

"Ow quit punching me." He punched him back.

"You know what's funny, I punched you like five times and you only punched me like three times."

"Oh so you want to make it even?" He punched him two more times but David dodged away.

"You don't know when to stop do you?"

"Not really." They struggled with each other once again.

"So, tell me again. How's your boyfriend doing?"

"Shut up. I don't have a boyfriend."

"Yeah right. He called me once."

"You have a girlfriend."

"I know I do. It's just he sounded nerdy on the phone. Does he where glasses or contacts or something?" Sean punched him. David laughed.

"Aha. So it is you have a boyfriend."

"Shut up." They walked up to the driveway.

"What's his name?"

"What you want me to hook him up with you or something?"

"Pff. I have a girlfriend. Besides, I don't swing that way man. I just want to know his name."

"I'm not telling you anything."

"Oh come on. I'm not going to tell anybody."

"No. Leave me alone." Sean took out his phone when he heard it vibrate.His eyes grew wide.

"What? Is it him? Does he want you to come over?" David had a smile on his face and laughed. He showed him and his eyes grew wide.

That was one thing that none of them expected. The only thing that they were to do was ignore it. But how could they?